STRICT CONFIDENCE

SKYE WARREN

CHAPTER ONE

Jane Mendoza

I DREAM ABOUT angels with white robes and talons for hands. They scratch at me, angry, accusing. I gasp against the pain. Flames lick at my skin. And all the while there's the voice, low and vibrating with fury. *I could have loved you,* it says.

Consciousness reaches down a hand and drags me up. It's like breaking the surface of the water—salt on my tongue and sea spray clouding my vision. It's too much. I can't move my arms or legs. Can't stay afloat. I cough into rising water.

Alone. I'm alone in this hazy, painful place.

"Hey," comes a voice. "Take it easy. Let's get you sitting up."

There's a mechanical whir, and then the world tilts. I look into concerned green eyes. A stranger. My waterlogged mind attempts to place him. I've seen him before.

My lips feel swollen as I mumble something. A greeting. A plea.

The nurse bustles around me, straightening the blanket. "Don't try to move. You're doing very well, but I want the doctor to sign off before you so much as sneeze."

I squeeze my eyes tight, trying to orient myself. Frantic moments at the hospital. A doctor shouting. The rest of the memories fall on me like a tidal wave.

Beau Rochester. The sex. The fire. The words he spoke in the inferno when I believed I was going to die: *I love you, damn you.*

A muted beep speeds up, and the nurse's face reappears. "Hey, now. No freaking out. You're going to be just fine. Some smoke inhalation. Some contusions. Let's not have a heart attack while you're under my care, please and thank you. You'll ruin my stats."

He keeps talking, so I can hear him, sense him, even though I can no longer see him. I like that he's got a touch of humor. It helps me focus on the current moment. The beeps slow down again. I guess that means I'm calm, but inside I feel frantic.

"Paige," I say, my voice hoarse.

"The little girl," comes the answer. "Two floors below us. She's going to be fine."

Relief washes over me. "Thank you."

"How long do you think it will take that handsome man of yours to get here? He insisted I text him as soon as you woke up, so I did. I'm guessing he skips the elevators. They're slow. No, he's probably climbing the stairs right now, which is not great for his leg, but does anyone listen to me? No, he's putting pressure on all the fractures which means that any minute now—"

"*Jane.*"

The pale hospital room fades into the background. The beeping quiets. The nurse retreats to his work, scribbling down notes on a clipboard that's attached to my hospital bed.

There's only him. Rochester. Dark eyes. A square jaw covered in a two-day beard. He looks rumpled and strong. But when he steps into the room, he limps. God, his leg was already messed up from the fall. It hadn't fully healed when the fire happened. It must hurt like crazy. I'm sure he shouldn't be walking around, but he is. He took the stairs to get to me as soon as I woke up. Something tightens in my chest.

"Are you okay?" I whisper.

Emotions flash through a stormy night gaze.

Relief. Guilt. And anger. It's the last one that holds my breath hostage. "Am I okay?" He makes a slashing motion with his hand. Then with visible effort he reins in whatever he's feeling. He strides over to me, his limp barely visible; I can tell he's trying to hide it. "I'm fine. The child in my custody almost died from a fire. And her nanny just woke up, when I thought she was going to—Yes. Fine."

My heart lurches. I remember his fury in the middle of the fire. His anguish that he couldn't force me to leave while he was pinned. "I'm sorry I didn't leave when you asked me to."

One dark eyebrow rises. "Are you?"

That's the worst part. I'm not really sorry, and he knows it. I would do it again in a heartbeat. How could I have left him to die? I know how it feels to be abandoned. I would never do that to him. "I'm sorry you're mad about it."

"Mad." A harsh laugh. The smoke inhalation affects him. His voice sounds like gravel. The exhaustion I feel must be affecting him, too, but he doesn't seem to show it. He's vibrant with anger. "Mad doesn't even touch what I'm feeling right now."

I want to ask more about how he's feeling, about whether he meant what he said. *I love you, damn you.* I search his expression, but I don't find any love there. Nothing soft or even kind. He looks as hard and as remote as the man I first met on the cliffside.

"The kitten," I gasp out.

"Safe and sound," he says. "Mateo's picking her up from the vet later."

"Who?"

One eyebrow raises. "Mateo Garza? The famous actor? I hope you didn't suffer memory loss, because I need you whole and healthy. We're checking out this afternoon."

The words are a slap in the face. I have to fight the physical recoil.

We're checking out this afternoon. Who? Him and Paige?

I'm still groggy from whatever's going through the IV attached to my hand. I can barely lift my head. Walking feels a million miles beyond my abilities.

That means he's leaving me behind. Where is the man who held me so tight it crushed my body? Where is the man who shouted that he loved me as if he could hold back the flames through force of will? He has the same dark eyes, the same square jaw. The same mahogany hair. Physically he's the same man. Emotionally he's a stranger.

"I'll be fine," I say around the knot in my throat.

It's habit that has me reassuring him, habit that comes from being alone and abandoned. Habit that I should have known better than to expect anything else.

In sixth grade the case worker was supposed to pick me up from one foster home and take me to a new one. She got delayed with another case. There was a phone call somewhere, a misplaced text, but the end result was that I sat on the curb in the blazing sun, sweat streaming down my face, running into my eyes.

And then it turned dark.

It got cold.

I huddled with my black trash bag full of clothes and schoolwork, waiting. I knew better than to go back inside the house. The door was locked. I didn't have a phone or any way to reach her, so I waited. I tore up blades of grass into thin slices. I dragged my finger along the rough pavement, trailing along after the ants and roly-polies who accepted me as one of them.

The case worker showed up the next morning, horrified that I'd been waiting.

I used the same voice then as I do now. The

same expression. False brightness. "I'll manage fine on my own. Don't worry about me."

Beau gives me an incredulous look. "Leave."

For a terrible second I think he's talking to me. The nurse shakes his head. Out of the corner of my eye I watch him walk out of the room, muttering under his breath.

I have a vague recollection of firefighters crashing into the room. They looked like martians in their huge yellow suits and helmets, wielding axes and hoses. There were EMTs who loaded me into an ambulance. A flurry of doctors when we arrived at the emergency room bay.

And then, when I woke up, there was the nurse.

I don't blame Rochester for not sitting with me. I understand he has his own injuries, his own exhaustion, though most likely he was with Paige. He has a responsibility to her. Of course he would stay with her, but it does mean this is the first time we've been together.

The first time we've been together since I thought I was going to die.

CHAPTER TWO

Beau Rochester

I KNOW I'M being churlish, but that knowledge isn't enough to stop me. Jane's eyes are red. Her voice is hoarse. There's a bruise on her temple and butterfly bandages beneath her lips. She's been injured, battered. I should be gentle, but I'm torn between sending her back to Houston or demanding she never, ever leave. I don't like feeling this out of control. She's got my emotions in a vise. Even with Emily, it was never like this.

"You're coming with us," I manage, my tone hard.

She blinks at me, those wide brown eyes that have seen too much pain for someone so young. I want to wrap my arms around her. "But what if the doctor—?"

"The doctor will discharge you. Unless you're

bleeding out, she's got better things to do than babysit you." *Stop being an ass, Rochester.* "Besides, Paige needs her nanny."

Jane's eyes are clouded with something— worry, hurt? I can't tell, but it's nothing good. It's nothing good because everything I say is wrong. "Of course. How is she? The nurse said she'll be okay, but how is she emotionally?"

A wreck. I don't say the words, because it feels like speaking them would make it real. I'd feel better if she raged and screamed and cried. Isn't that normal behavior for a child who experienced trauma? Instead she's withdrawing. The nurses and doctors on her floor wear colorful scrubs with cartoon characters. They have stickers and other fun things in their pockets, but she glares at them with blatant mistrust. And Mateo. She can barely stand to be in the same room with him. I shouldn't have guilted Jane into coming home with us, but it was the truth. Paige does need her nanny. I need her nanny, too.

I clear my throat. "She'll manage. You shouldn't feel obligated to leave with us, of course. Facing a house fire wasn't part of your employment contract. If you want to leave, I'll understand. I can have a car pick you up from the hospital and take you directly to the airport."

Jane swallows. "Is that what you want? Do you want me to leave?"

No. I'm not even sure I could let you. If you tell me you want to leave, I might have to tie you to the hospital bed with plastic tubing to keep you here. They'll lock me up, and then who will take care of Paige? "You almost died, for God's sake."

"I didn't think you'd be this angry," she says in a small, halting voice.

How can I explain? It felt like blades tearing my skin into strips. I would have burned a thousand times over rather than hold her, clutched in my arms, my hands uselessly covering her head against falling, burning debris, knowing she would perish. I'm not angry; I'm fucking insane with worry. Even thirty-six hours later, I still feel it.

Years ago I fell in love with a woman. I could afford to take that plunge, even if it nearly drowned me. I can't do it again. Not only for my own sake. I can't do it because Paige needs me. She needs me whole and sane—and numb. Numb to this emotion.

"A bonus," I say. "There was no house fire clause in the contract, but it's only fair. If you decide to stay on with Paige, you'll receive a sizable bonus."

Tears fill her eyes, but they don't fall. They hover there, dancing on her dark lashes. "I'm not leaving Paige. A bonus isn't necessary."

"Here's a tip," I say, my voice caustic. "If your employer offers you a bonus, take it."

"Right," she says, her voice hollow.

I know I'm being a patronizing asshole. Someone should take me out behind the hospital and kick the shit out of me. Maybe Mateo will do it later. He probably owes me an ass kicking for something. Then again, my leg hurts bad enough already. Maybe that's my penance for being an asshole. This throbbing sensation that will never go away.

But I can't act fucking normal about this. I was in her bed when the fire started. Would it still have happened if I hadn't been obsessed with her sweet pussy? The thought haunts me. Did I cause the fire by fucking the nanny? I can't let it happen again.

"What we did that night... what we did before..."

"Sex," she says, her head high, her chin quivering. She won't let me shame her.

Good girl. "That's right. Sex. It won't happen again."

She tugs at the coarse white sheet that covers

her, using it as a shield. Because she needs protection. From me. It wrenches my stomach. "Okay," she says.

"It's not that you aren't beautiful. You are. It's—"

"Let me guess," she says, her voice quivering. "It's not me, it's you."

"Correct." It's not her. She's beautiful and smart and kind. She has a whole life ahead of her. Meanwhile I'm a selfish bastard who used her. The fire was a disaster in ten different ways, but there is one small, shining upside. It was also a wake-up call that I desperately needed.

She manages a wry, watery smile. "Don't worry, Beau. I hear you loud and clear. And I respect your boundaries. I'm not going to take advantage of you."

Oh the fucking irony. And worse, she knows it. She knows that I was using her. It's a little joke at my expense, and I deserve it. What can I say to that sharp awareness? What can I do but fall to my knees and beg her forgiveness? I won't be able to last a day without her in my arms. I won't be able to watch her without wanting her.

"Jane. I'm dangerous to you. Look at what happened to Emily. Now look at you, almost burned to a crisp in a fire, small and fragile in a hospital bed—because of me." Her brow furrows, and I know she means to argue with me. "God, I'm not even good for Paige. You know it. You said it yourself. I snap at her. I argue with her. I'm the problem here."

Her eyes fill with tears. "You love me. You said you love me."

It would be better to deny it, to claim I didn't mean it, but I can't quite bring myself to lie to her that way. "It doesn't matter. My love is dangerous."

There's a knock at the door.

A woman in a white lab coat. Dr. Gupta. I met her earlier. Made an ass out of myself swearing at her and then pleading with her, demanding that she promise Jane would be okay.

She gives me a patient smile and then turns to Jane. "You're awake. Good. How do you feel?"

"Tired," Jane says, offering a wan smile. God, she's strong. And brave. I want to shield her from the world, which is cruel and dangerous. I want to shield her from me.

"Of course you are," Dr. Gupta says, lifting a chart to make some notes. "Fatigue will last for a couple weeks. Your body needs time to heal. And how about the pain?"

Jane's gaze darts to me, and my throat tightens. I'm causing her pain. "I'm fine," she says in that deceptively real way. It sounds true, but it isn't. "Though I haven't gotten out of bed yet. I'm a little worried about how that's going to go."

Dr. Gupta frowns. "You won't be getting out of bed unassisted for a few days."

"We're leaving this afternoon."

The doctor glances at the window where dawn has crept through the cheap plastic blinds. "Leaving to go where? Scuba diving? Rock climbing? I don't think so."

My chest squeezes. The pediatrician already told me he's ready to release Paige. What will happen if Paige leaves? I'll go with her. Of course I will. I've never thought about death. Never worried about it. Never feared it. Not because I believed I was invincible. The water taught us early that we didn't control our fate. I didn't fear it because part of me would welcome the quiet deep. Not anymore. Not now that Paige depends on me. If I had died in that fire, I couldn't protect Paige. Even Jane couldn't have gotten custody of her. No, I know my responsibility lies with that child.

But that will leave Jane alone in the hospital.

I already see the panic in her dark eyes, though she tries to hide it. I'm a bastard in ten different ways, but I refuse to leave her in this cold, sterile room. "You have a few hours, Doctor. Use them however you want. Treat her. Drug her. Operate on her, if you want, but this afternoon, we're getting the hell out of here."

CHAPTER THREE

Jane Mendoza

I'T'S ONLY AFTER Beau has left, after the doctor has done a thorough examination, that I'm completely alone. That's when it hits me—the gravity of my situation. For years I dragged around my belongings in a trash bag. Everything I wore was threadbare and too small. I thought that was the low point in my life. Rock bottom.

I was wrong. Rock bottom? It's right now.

The family I thought I'd found, the love I held in my hand for a matter of seconds… Gone.

My love is dangerous. I'm alone, which has always been my deepest, darkest fear.

I'm in a generic hospital room. There is no phone on the bedside table, no jacket slung over a chair. No *Get Well Soon* balloon beating against the ceiling tiles. Nothing to show that anyone stays here. It could be unoccupied if it weren't for me. It almost feels like I'm not really here. As if I could disappear. The world wouldn't notice.

The carry-on luggage I found at Goodwill was threadbare, but it was mine. It contained everything I own. And now it's gone. Burned up in a fire.

My breath comes faster. And then not at all. I'm gasping, clenching my fingers in the coarse white sheets, pressing my face to the pillow.

Panic. The word shoots through my mind like a comet, bright and hot.

It feels like there's a vise around my throat, but I force myself to breathe in air. It's made of knives, the air. I drag them into my lungs. Tears burn my eyes.

I remember a coping technique one of the therapists taught us in group sessions.

Five things I can see. My hospital gown, white with light blue dots. Black scuff marks on a white rubber floor. Beige plastic trim around the base of the room, cracked at the edges. My nails, dark with soot beneath them. Scrapes on the palms of my hands.

Four things I can touch. My hospital gown, thin and abrasive. The blanket that covers me. Plastic railings that keep me in bed. Tape holding an IV to my hand, the edges curling off my skin.

Three things I can hear. A steady *beep beep beep* from the machines. The murmur of the nurses in their station outside my room. Far away, laughter from a daytime TV show.

Two things I can smell. Antiseptic. And brown sugar.

One thing I can taste—oatmeal.

There's a tray of cooling hospital food on the tray beside me. The doctor left me with strict orders to eat something. I force myself to take a bite of the thick brown sugar oatmeal and swallow, though it barely registers as flavor. I don't know whether that's a commentary on the cafeteria or on my emotional state. Probably both.

A knock at the door.

It's already half-open. A white man in a black suit and severe expression walks inside, not waiting for a response to his knock. "Ms. Mendoza?"

"That's me." My voice comes out scratchy. More than that, it hurts. It feels like someone's sifting pieces of sandpaper against my vocal cords. I don't want to talk to anyone, but I especially don't want to talk to this person. A stranger. An intimidating one.

"Detective Joe Causey." He doesn't reach to shake my hand. Either he's read the doctor's report about how they're scratched up or he just doesn't do that. He pulls out a small notepad and pen. "I'm looking into the fire at the Rochester place."

I glance at the notepad, where he's already started scribbling something. I haven't even said anything yet. What's he writing down? "Wouldn't that be the fire department?"

"The fire chief called me out at two o'clock in the morning to take a look at the scene."

"Oh." Maybe that's why he looks so severe. He got no sleep. Technically I also got very little sleep, but I can't imagine sleeping. I feel frantic and jumpy. After all, the fire started when I was asleep. Slumber doesn't feel safe anymore. As if it's sleep that led to the flames and the smoke. As if it's sleep, instead of the fire, that's the enemy.

"Just a few questions. Your name is Jane Mendoza. You work for the family. Is that correct?"

"Yes. I'm the nanny for Paige."

"And last night. What time did you have dinner?"

"Six, maybe? Seven? It was my day off, so they made spaghetti without me." Beau and Paige were dancing in the kitchen when I got home from town.

"So you didn't cook."

"No."

"Did you go back to the kitchen after you ate? Make anything else?"

"Why would that—" Something catches at the back of my throat and I cough. It hurts. "I didn't, but why would that—"

"Most accidental fires start in the kitchen. Sometimes, looking back, a person might remember leaving the stove on."

"I didn't leave the stove on."

"And where were you when you first noticed the fire?"

"I noticed the smoke." I noticed the heat, actually. In my dreams. "It woke me up. Smoke in my bedroom. I'm not sure what time it was."

It was after we had sex.

"So you didn't go back to the kitchen. You were around the house, going to bed—"

"Yes. We put Paige to bed, and I went to my room, and when I woke up—"

"Alone?"

I'm not trying to be difficult, it's just that there's a clamor in my head. A sense of urgency running through my veins. I don't know this person. Detective? Yes. Sure. In my world, police were the people that pulled you away from your parents. They were the people who looked the other way when foster parents were abusive. "What does this have to do with the fire?"

"I'm trying to get the facts, ma'am." He seems to set aside the original question. "How long have you been working for Beau Rochester?"

Ma'am. That's the first time I've ever been called that. The word is meant to be respectful, but the way he says it feels combative. It's mocking me because I'm not really in a position of respect. I'm nobody. "A few months. I think." I rub my forehead. "I'm not sure. If I check my email, I would know. I don't have my phone. It was... in the fire."

"And how much time do you spend with the family?"

"Most of my time. Like I said, I'm Paige's nanny, so I'm there all the time, except for my days off." I have a vision of this gruff, serious man questioning Paige and my heart speeds up. "Did you talk to her? Is she okay?"

"I spoke with Beau—" He catches himself. "With Mr. Rochester already."

That makes me blink. The way he said Beau was casual. Personal. As if he knows him. "Mr. Rochester grew up around here. He said that once."

A pause. And then a short nod. "We went to school together."

What was he like? It's like I have a window to his childhood right now. "High school? Middle school? How long have you known him?"

He ignores this. "What made you accept the job?"

The words rise in my throat. *Well, you see, Detective, the world requires us to work in order to buy things. Like food.* I force down my defiance. "I'm saving up for college, but I don't see how that's related to the fire."

"Would you describe your relationship with Beau Rochester as strictly professional?"

My pulse spikes. A thin neon line on a black screen jumps. "That's none of your business."

"This is a police investigation. I need you to answer my questions, even if they don't feel comfortable to you. And we met in elementary school."

I open my mouth. And close it. Something deep inside tells me not to trust this man. I don't like the hard look in his eyes or the presumptive way he speaks. But I don't know if that fear is coming from my past, from a lifetime of not trusting authority.

Or if it's good, old-fashioned PTSD from the

fire.

"I live in the same house," I say cautiously. "We see each other every day. We have dinner together. There's a natural closeness for a live-in nanny that I didn't expect when I took the job. So I don't know whether I'd call it strictly professional."

A memory rises, the dark shadow of Mr. Rochester above me.

"Tell me to stop," he mutters against my lips.

It's already a kiss, those words. I close my eyes. A tear leaks down the side of my cheek. It's not sadness. It's more than that. It's desire. It's feeling anything at all after being numb for so long. I'm more afraid of this than a free fall down the cliff. "Don't stop."

"Fuck," he says, wrapping his hand around my throat. Choking me, but without the pressure. It doesn't hurt, but it makes me feel strange, as if I'm being possessed. "You're too innocent for the things I want to do to you."

"What do you want to do to me?"

"Everything."

My cheeks burn. I'm sure they must be pink right now, but I force myself to keep meeting the detective's pale blue eyes. "I see," he murmurs, and I have the disturbing sense that he does see. "He's driven. Always has been. I suppose you could say we have that in common, with one key difference. I always wanted to make something of myself right here."

"And he went to California."

"His own personal Gold Rush, you could say."

There are undercurrents in his voice. Jealousy? Resentment? I suppose it would be hard to see someone he considered a peer become a rich man. I'm not immune to envy. There were times I wanted a sandwich and fruit roll-ups instead of a hot lunch I paid for with a free lunch number. Times I wanted a birthday party or gymnastic lessons or all the other things girls in my class got to have. Jealous feelings don't make me particularly noble, but they do make me human.

"Do you hate him?" I ask.

He gives me an impassive look. "Until very recently I didn't think much about him at all. Though I was curious to find out why he had a nineteen-year-old nanny living under his roof." He checks his notepad, though I get the sense he isn't really reading anything. "And I understand you slept across the hall from him. That's… close."

"This has nothing to do with the fire."

"The fire chief believes it might be arson."

Shock runs through my system. "I still don't see what this has to do with the fire."

"Where were you when the fire started?"

"You think I set it?"

"I think there were three people in the house when it started. I intend to question all of them."

"Why would I set a fire? What possible reason could I have to do that?"

"Now that's an interesting question. It's one I'm sure I'll be thinking about. A fight between lovers, perhaps. Did you think Rochester would marry you?"

A laugh of disbelief escapes me. "You have no idea what you're talking about."

"Maybe you thought you'd get his money. You and Beau are both alike. A girl like you would fuck him for money and set his house on fire."

My heart pounds at the sudden change in tone. This isn't the coldly professional detective who walked in. This is someone else, someone with a personal stake in his questions. There's a heavy feeling in my stomach. Shock. And dread. "I almost died in that fire."

"But you didn't."

My head shakes, back and forth, back and forth. It's scary to think that someone might have set that fire. Who could have done it? Paige was asleep in her room. And Mr. Rochester was in bed… with me. Technically we both have an alibi. We couldn't have set the fire because we were beneath the same sheet, limbs tangled together, sated. I don't say any of that to Detective Causey, though. He already seems suspicious of my relationship with Beau.

"Listen," I say, my voice shaking. "I understand you have to ask questions and investigate, but I would gain nothing if Beau or Paige died in a fire. I don't have any anger against either of them. They've been like a family to me."

The detective nods as if he expected as much, as if he didn't just make that ugly accusation. "That leaves the other people in the house, then. Paige doesn't present as a sociopath, so that leaves Beau Rochester. Did you know that the most common motive of arson is to commit insurance fraud?"

A vise closes around my lungs. "Why would he do that?"

The detective gives me a cold smile. The hair on the back of my neck rises. Living in group homes, you get a sense for danger. You know which people never to turn your back on. He's one of them. "Why not? Because he's wealthy?

There's never enough money, Ms. Mendoza. And once you've acquired a taste for making it, it's hard to stop."

"Are you speaking from experience?" I ask, my voice hoarse.

I don't know where the accusation comes from. Detectives don't exactly make tons of money, do they? Except I had the feeling he *was* speaking from experience. His eyes narrow. "We'll all do things we aren't proud of for the right price, won't we?"

My heart thumps in my chest. If he knew about my intimate relationship with Mr. Rochester, I'm sure he would accuse me of sleeping with him for money. I swallow around the lump in my throat. "Not everything we do is for money."

A hard smile. "You're young, Ms. Mendoza. Perhaps you still believe that."

There's a bustle outside. Shouting. Then Beau bursts into the room, his nostrils flaring, his dark eyes blazing. "What the hell are you doing in here?"

The room was tense before—a spill of gasoline. Beau Rochester is the match.

"Just doing my job," Detective Causey says with deceptive calm. Deceptive because I can sense the challenge underneath his words. It's a glint in his blue eyes.

Beau's wearing a casual beige jacket over a white T-shirt and jeans. He brings with him the crisp smell of the Maine outdoors. Along with the faint scent of something burnt. That's when I realize he must have just come from visiting the Coach House. He hides the limp; his fury overcoming whatever pain he feels from walking around.

I narrow my eyes at Causey. "You said you just spoke to Beau."

"I told you I'd spoken with him already. I never said I spoke with him about the fire."

"Listen, Causey," Beau says, his voice pitched low, fury vibrating through every syllable. "You don't speak to her. You don't speak to Paige. You have a question for them? Ask me."

That makes Causey smile. It's not a nice smile. "Protecting your employee? That's admirable. I wasn't sure you had it in you. Figured you'd throw her to the wolves."

"Go to hell," Beau says, the words a growl.

"Then again, maybe you aren't so much protecting her. Maybe you're keeping the family secrets. Secrets she's been learning while she lives under your roof."

"Leave." Beau stands between the hospital bed and the detective, as if he really is protecting me. Against what? An overzealous detective? A childhood rivalry? It feels worse than that. Deeper than that, though I can't see the undercurrents. I can only feel them. "Don't come back without a warrant. We have nothing to say to you."

"Or what?" Causey asks, taking a step toward Beau. Toward me.

"Or I'll have your fucking badge."

A harsh laugh. "You may have been hot shit in California. With your money and your women. But you're still the Rochester kid around here. I don't have a goddamn IPO but I have all the connections I could need around here. You can't touch me."

I watch in stunned silence while Causey leaves the hospital room.

Beau turns to me, his dark eyes intense. "What did he say to you?" His hard gaze sweeps over my hospital-gown-covered body. "Did he hurt you? Did he touch you?"

Touch me? Maybe the detective's line of questioning was rude. Even aggressive, but he didn't touch me. "Of course not. Why was he so... angry?"

"I have no idea," Beau says, his voice grim. It

29

sounds like a lie.

My stomach turns. Why did Detective Causey lie about talking to Beau before? Did he think I'd be more likely to let something slip? Why is Beau lying to me now? I'm walking through a spiderweb, blind to the strands, trapped by their strength.

The scent of burnt wafts wood over me again, along with the memories. Smoke. Flames. Being trapped in the house, believing I would die. "How's the house?" I manage to ask.

Beau runs a hand through his hair. He looks stressed. Distracted. Of course he is. His house just burned to the ground. And I know his leg must be killing him even if he manages to hide it. I can't believe Causey even suggested Beau might be responsible. "Not great. It's a crime scene until the investigation's closed, so we can't even begin repairs."

"Where will we stay?" As soon as the words are out of my mouth, I wish I could take them back. There may not be a *we* anymore. For all I know he's going to send me back to Houston.

"That's what I was coming here to tell you. Mateo found us a place. The hospital's discharging you and Paige right now. We're going."

CHAPTER FOUR

Beau Rochester

I SCAN THE parking lot, but there's no sign of Joe Causey. He's a detective now. I hadn't even heard he'd joined the police force, but it makes sense.

Bullies like power.

And Joe Causey was always a bully.

Paige stands on a small patch of grass, clutching a pink teddy bear from the hospital gift shop. The stuffed animal looks large against her slender body. She wears a plain white T-shirt with the logo of the hospital and a pair of generic, too-large sweatpants that bunch up at her feet. It makes me feel protective. And royally pissed. How dare Causey try to question her without me? Thank fuck for Mateo. He sat with her for the hour it took to meet the fire chief at the house. He managed to hold off the hospital staff from letting

Causey inside.

How did Causey know I'd be gone? Coincidence? Not likely. I've been by Paige's side nonstop, only taking breaks to go to the bathroom or check on Jane. One of the only times I step outside the hospital, that's when Causey shows up.

He's probably friends with a nurse or a doctor here.

A black Escalade pulls up to the curb. The black-tinted window rolls down. Mateo looks at me over the top of his sunglasses. "Someone ordered an Uber?"

"Thanks, man," I say, my voice pitched low. "I owe you one. Or two. Or three."

He gets out and circles the vehicle.

Paige sidles close to me. She doesn't trust Mateo, even though she met him at the dinner party. She doesn't trust anyone since the fire. Doctors, nurses, all of them suspect. Even the balloon artist who made the rounds in the pediatric ward was subject to her glare.

"Hey, Paige," Mateo says with a small wave.

She hides her face against my jeans.

"We appreciate your help," I say, more for her benefit.

He gives a small smile, letting us know he

doesn't take offense to her rebuff. "The inn is all ready for you. You have rooms right next door to each other. They overlook the water."

She ignores him.

"Wait here with Mateo," I tell Paige, gently detaching her. "I need to get Jane."

There's a whoosh of air behind me. Large sliding doors open. An orderly pushes a wheelchair out. Jane blinks against the sun. She's also wearing hospital-issued clothing, since she showed up in fire-torn nightclothes. She looks small and far too skinny sitting there. Delicate. *Breakable.*

Worry fights with frustration inside me. "I told you to wait for me. I was going to come get you."

She gives me a wan smile that's supposed to be reassuring. "This was easier." Then she turns to Paige. "Hey, sweetheart. How are you?"

Paige gives a diffident shrug. Gone is the girl who grinned at Jane, who challenged her, who painted every rock and tree and surface in sight. Now there's only a shadow.

There's a flash of hurt across Jane's face. Then she covers it up. She's exactly the nanny Paige needs. The care she deserves. How could I have risked that by sleeping with Jane? How can I keep Jane in Maine, knowing I've put her in danger?

She could have died. The best thing would be for me to send her back to Houston.

You'd never see her again. The thought whispers through my head, the faint scent of salt on an ocean breeze. It's selfishness that keeps her here. My selfishness.

She's so strong. It breaks my heart that I need her to be strong. Part of me wants to sweep her away to some island paradise, far away from the cold, drizzly cliffs. Far away from the fire. Paige needs me. I made a promise to her when her parents died.

And there's an ongoing investigation into the fire.

Instead of sweeping her away to an island paradise, I help her stand.

She trembles slightly in my grasp before shooing me away. "I'm fine," she says with only a fraction of her normal voice. It's shaken her, that fire.

It's shaken both her body and her spirit.

Her dark lashes lower. She sways gently. It's Mateo who's there to catch her, to escort her to the passenger seat. "Hey, now. Careful. Don't worry. I'm not a superhero, but I play one on TV."

"I thought you're in movies," Jane says, her

voice faint with thread of humor.

He acts offended. "You thought? *You thought?* Does that mean you haven't seen my movies?" He continues teasing her as he helps her into the SUV.

I have to bite back the urge to warn him away. *Don't touch her. She's mine.* There's no room for caveman antics, not when I have responsibilities.

"Come on," I say, leading Paige to the other side. "Hop in."

She frowns, clearly thinking about stalling. Then she hesitantly lifts her hands. She's been in a mood since the fire. I can't exactly blame her. I settle her into a bucket seat and lock the seat belt into place. Then I climb into the backseat beside her, holding back my wince as my leg protests. It's stiff and throbbing. The crutches I got after the fall, the cane I sometimes used—all of them were consumed by the fire. Which is just fine with me. I could have gotten new ones, but I don't want them. I don't need them. I was caught unaware once. It won't happen again.

Mateo guides the Escalade out of the hospital parking lot and onto the road.

"I'm hungry," Paige says when we reach the highway.

"We'll have dinner soon," I say, even though

it's only three p.m.

"I'm hungry *now*."

I glance at her. She isn't usually this demanding. And I happen to know she ate the entire burger we got from the cafeteria for lunch. I don't think she's hungry, but she needs… something. Reassurance maybe, though I don't know how to provide that.

"Mac and cheese," she adds in an imperious tone.

I hesitate. It's been hard enough figuring out a place to stay, somewhere safe and secure, dealing with the officials. Hard enough without also making sure the kitchen would have her particular essentials. "Maybe they can make mac and cheese. We'll ask."

Feather-light blonde eyebrows rise. "We'll ask who?"

"The innkeeper."

"I thought we were going home."

"No," I say gently. "Remember we talked about this? Home is going to need work. Construction work. It will take a long time. In the meantime, we're going to stay at the inn."

Her face turns red. I've seen this color before. Exactly one time before.

We were at the wake for her parents. She had

made it through the funeral with grave obedience. *Stand here. Walk there. Say goodbye.* All the times when I would have expected her to rage, she held her composure. It was only at the end, when families gathered at the Coach House, when they offered empty words of consolation and casseroles, that she lost it.

"Get out," she had screamed, her face red and splotchy, tears leaking down her cheeks. No one could console her. No one could reprimand her. In the end they left, one by one, darting glances of worry between me and her. In the hollow house, once everyone had gone, she beat her fists against me and sobbed into my chest for hours. Until she fell asleep in my arms.

She looks the same way now. Mutinous. Angry.

Consumed by grief.

"I want Kitten."

"She's at the vet, remember? We'll pick her up soon."

"I want mac and cheese. And I want to go home."

Despite my general ineptitude as a guardian, I've tried. I've read books and listened to podcasts. Don't raise your voice, they say. Lower your voice, and the child will mimic you. "We can't go home," I say, my words quiet. "There's yellow tape everywhere. It's a crime scene."

This, despite the books and the podcasts, is the wrong thing to say. I know it when her eyes turn wide. I see the whites around her blue pupils. Her little nostrils flare. "No," she says. "No. *No*. I'm not going anywhere else. I'm going home."

We're seconds away from the edge. I can see the waterfall—the long drop and the sharp rocks at the bottom, but I don't have a fucking paddle.

Jane turns back in her seat, her dark hair falling like silk over her shoulder. "Paige," she says. That's all. *Paige*. There's a wealth of emotion in that one word. Sorrow and sympathy.

Paige's lower lip trembles. "I hate this."

"Yes," Jane says.

"I don't want to stay at a hotel. I want to go home."

"You want to go home," Jane says. "Where it's safe. Because you're afraid."

"You don't understand," Paige says, her voice wavering.

"Then tell me," Jane says, coaxing. "Why do you want to go home?"

"If I'm not there, my mommy won't know where to find me."

The whispered words make my throat tighten.

Christ. As if the child didn't have enough to worry about with a goddamn fire destroying her home and belongings. She also thinks her mother's coming back? I'd fight a goddamn army for her. I'd dive under an eighteen-wheeler if it would keep her safe, but I can't protect her from false hope.

"Your mother always knows where you are," Jane says, reaching back. After a short pause, Paige holds her hand. They stay like that, linked. "She loves you, wherever she is. Wherever you are. Nothing can stop that. Not a fire, not the ocean, nothing."

A sniffle. A sob. And then Paige does break.

She doesn't scream at everyone to leave her house. Instead she cries quiet tears, her small hand clenched around Jane's so hard her knuckles turn white, as if Jane is the only steady thing in a stormy sea. It's an awkward position, Jane turned around in the passenger seat, but she doesn't try to right herself. Instead she rests her forehead against the leather seat, a tear sliding down her cheek. This is a bond they share, both of them orphaned. It doesn't matter that I love Paige like my own daughter. Or that I've fallen for Jane. This is something outside my experience. They're both grieving right now. Both finding hope in that tether.

They stay that way the entire ride to the inn, Paige quietly drowning, Jane keeping her afloat. I can only watch from the outside, useless, unable to protect either one of them. I wasn't lying when I told Jane it wasn't her. It's me. My love is dangerous. It's dangerous to Jane. It's dangerous to Paige. I should keep my distance from Paige for her own sake.

This feels like more than a moment. It feels like a portend.

Like the fire was only the beginning.

Someone may have set the fire in that house. The fire chief suspects as much. I have no idea who lit a match, but I know one thing: There were no bodies found in the charred remains.

Whoever set the fire is still out there.

CHAPTER FIVE

Jane Mendoza

F ROM THE OUTSIDE, the Lighthouse Inn looks like a large cottage. White columns hold up a wraparound balcony. Thick ivy with purple flowers climbs up the side. A picket fence guards the grassy path down to the beach. Once you get up close, once you get inside, it feels less like a cottage. There are no embroidered pillows or roughened wood surfaces. Dark wood planks on the floor gleam. Waterford crystal glasses sit beside a pitcher of cucumber water. The owner, a slender woman named Marjorie, checks us in personally. She comes around the marble countertop to shake Beau's hand.

She drops to a knee in front of Paige. "Hi, sweetheart. Would you like anything? Perhaps some hot chocolate? Or some fresh sugar cookies?"

Paige turns her face into my stomach, hiding. It's to her credit that Marjorie doesn't look angry at the rebuff. But she does give me a curious glance. And then one at Beau. There's a knot in my throat. Is she speculating that something's happening between us? It feels like there's a scarlet letter A on my clothes, especially after the detective made his accusations.

Meanwhile Beau looks impervious. The limp is barely noticeable. He glances around the lobby with a remote expression. "The security team finished working?"

A series of expressions flit across Marjorie's delicate features: worry, tension, shame. "They installed a whole system. Have this place locked up tighter than Fort Knox."

My heart thuds a warning. A security system? I turn to face Beau. My voice sounds strange to my own ears. "Why would we need a security system?"

"It's always good to be safe," he says, his tone nonchalant.

Before I can question him further, Mateo comes in from the outside with a gust of cold air. "I'm heading to the mall after this to restock your wardrobes, so let me know if you have any special requests."

"No," I say, whirling.

Everyone stops and faces me. The large space becomes quiet. There's a *tick tick tick* from an ornate grandfather clock. It feels like this is spinning out of control.

"You can't buy me new clothes," I say, fighting to sound calm over the beating of blood in my ears. I felt calm enough when we were leaving the hospital, but I didn't understand.

I couldn't understand how much everything would change until I was standing here, about to sleep in a room I've never seen, about to wear clothes that aren't mine. About to become a different person.

It's like I really died in that fire. Someone else stands here now.

Not Jane Mendoza. A stranger.

Concern darkens Mateo's eyes, but he doesn't respond. Marjorie looks away as if she's embarrassed for me. Beau wears that same impassive expression I'm coming to hate. It made sense when I was new to Maine. He didn't know me then. Now he's held me close, trying to shield my body with his own. He told me loved me, but he stands there as aloof as… an employer. That's what he is to me. My boss.

There's a tug on my hand. I look down. Paige

wears a solemn expression. "They burned in the fire. Your old clothes. Uncle Beau explained it to me. They're gone."

Maybe I look ridiculous for making a stand over clothes. They're just things, right? It's just that they're my only possessions in the entire world. My only heritage. Our lives are the most important thing. We made it out, safe and sound.

Reassurance comes from Paige's eyes, blue as the sky.

"You're right," I manage to say. "Of course you're right. Thank you, Mateo, for getting me clothes. And for getting us rooms here. I'll pay you back."

Mateo shakes his head. "It will go on a Rochester credit card. Black, of course."

Beau won't look at me. It's not my imagination. Part of me wondered if he'd been avoiding my gaze, but now I'm sure of it. He stares at the wall, as if the hunter green lace wallpaper pattern holds the secrets of the universe.

"Then I'll pay you back," I say, willing him to look at me.

Then he does, his dark gaze so full of torment that my breath catches. It's not that he doesn't care. It's that he's overfull with it, brimming with worry and anguish and fear. It simmers at the heart of him, as hot as the fire we barely escaped, smoke filling my lungs.

He doesn't say no. He doesn't have to. It's there in the room, his refusal. His challenge. *Don't even try to pay me back. I won't let you.* He doesn't know how badly I need to stand on equal footing with him, how much I need to not owe him. Clothes aren't part of the compensation package. If I let him buy me clothes, then I let myself become a whore.

"Well," says Marjorie, still with that embarrassed half smile, not quite meeting my eyes. I'm the crazy one in her eyes. She's not even wrong. "I'm sure Beau Rochester can afford a few pairs of jeans. I read the article about him in Forbes. Can you believe it? A fisherman's son."

"The room keys," he says, his voice soft, almost menacing. He doesn't acknowledge her gushing. Does it make him uncomfortable? It feels like something deeper is going on.

Pink floods Marjorie's cheeks. "Of course. I have them right here. All of you are on the second floor to give you privacy. Mateo's already set up in one of the rooms on the right. Beachfront rooms, of course. All of them. Breakfast is at eight a.m.... well, usually it is. Normally we're rather strict about it, but I suppose now that you've rented out the entire inn, we can do it whenever works best for you."

He rented the entire inn? There must be twenty guest rooms here. I looked it up when the dinner party happened. One room is expensive. I can't imagine how much the entire place costs. And the fire only happened three days ago. It's beautiful by the beach. Prime tourist season. Only now the empty parking lot registers. "Didn't you have reservations?"

She waves a hand. "We moved them to the Black Point Resort down the coast. A beautiful place, of course. Not quite as nice as mine, but they will be well taken care of—especially with the resort credit Beau gave them. The spa is extremely nice."

It's still hard to wrap my head around this amount of money. I knew he was wealthy, of course. I knew he was successful, but it's another level to see it in action. To see him change around the plans of other couples, other families, simply because he's… rich.

Another tug on my hand. Paige looks worried now. "This is okay, isn't it?"

Concern shines in her blue eyes. It's almost like she thinks I might leave. That if I don't like the arrangements, I'd leave. *And wouldn't I? I'm not bound to this family by anything more than an employment contract. It works both ways. He can fire me tomorrow, but I can just as easily quit.* I drop to one knee so that I'm actually lower than her, looking up into her sweet face. There's not even a single scratch from the fire. Beau got her out quickly enough. "I'm not going anywhere," I promise her. "We're going to be very comfortable here. And very safe."

Over her shoulder I meet Beau's dark eyes. There's a flicker before he turns away. As if he doesn't think it's a promise I can keep. My heart thuds against my ribs.

What danger are we in?

The peace doesn't last long.

Paige tolerates the large bed with its chenille bedspread and creaky antique chairs.

She becomes ominously silent when she sees the tray of food that's been sent up with sandwiches with cucumber, cream cheese, and dill. There's also strawberry and basil scones. And a creamy mushroom soup.

She refuses to try it. Any of it. I'm coaxing her to take a bite of the scone when there's a knock at the door. Mateo stands there, his arms loaded with large white shopping bags with the *Nordstrom* logo. "Personal delivery," he says with that billion-dollar grin.

My eyes widen. I've never seen so many purchases in one single haul. I don't really have a history with shopping bags. I've usually worn hand-me-downs or state-issued clothes. "All this?" I ask, my voice faint. "Is some of it for Beau?"

"Nah, I'll bring his up in a second." He lifts one muscular shoulder. "Sorry if I picked the wrong stuff. I grabbed everything that seemed like it would fit. We'll have to go back when it gets cold, but this should do you through the summer."

He leaves in a whirlwind of masculine energy, leaving us alone with the bags.

Paige and I exchange a look fraught with concern.

I put on a fake, cheerful smile and open the first one. There's a selection of short-sleeve shirts in a rainbow of colors—heather gray and navy blue and pale blush. They're only T-shirts. I've worn a thousand of them before, but they were never like this. Velvety soft. Somehow thicker and more substantial than anything I've had before. Still light as a feather. The price tag makes my heart skip a beat. He paid this... *per shirt.*

He has to return them. There's no way I could ever pay Beau back for these. I rub the lush fabric between my thumb and forefinger. For a moment I pull it against my chest, imagining wearing it, imagining being the kind of woman who belongs here.

The fantasy shatters when Paige opens a different bag.

She pulls out a pile of dresses that look like they'd fit her perfectly. They're the right size... but wrong in every other way. These are girlish and playful with winking unicorn emojis and hot pink ruffles. "These aren't my clothes," she says, her voice shaky like she's about to cry.

"I thought you knew," I say softly. "I thought Uncle Beau explained."

"He said my clothes were gone. The one with the grape jelly stain and the jeans with a hole that I cut myself. He said I'd get new clothes. I thought they'd be like the old ones." There's grief in her voice. Those Monopoly T-shirts she loved. The black tulle skirt.

She loved her clothes, and they're gone. They're gone.

My clothes weren't nearly so cool. I picked them up at Goodwill and Walmart, but they were mine. The only shelter that came with me from foster home to my own apartment to Maine.

Clothes are more than objects. They were part

of me. An extension of my body. Part of my identity in a world that so often forgets that I exist. Paige understands, because she's like me. We have this in common. We're transients in this world, without a place of our own.

"I'm sorry," I whisper, and her chin wobbles.

I try to give her a hug, but she turns her face away.

She holds it together until it's time to take a bath. She takes one step onto the marble tile and freezes. The copper clawfoot tub gleams in the bright light. Her chin lifts. "*What* is *that*?"

"It's a bathtub. Like the one you have back home." As soon as the words leave my lips, I know they're the wrong thing to say. The one she has back home has been burned to a crisp. Then again, I'm not sure there is any right thing to say in this situation.

Tears glisten from her eyes. "Why does it look like that?"

Her voice has turned shrill, and I make mine soothing. "It has feet, see? To make it higher. It's really pretty. A little bit old fashioned but beautiful."

"I can't even see inside. How can I get in? I'll drown!"

It is definitely higher than her tub at home.

"I'll find a step stool," I tell her. "I'm sure there's a step stool somewhere here. And we won't make the water go to the top."

Watching this meltdown is like watching a volcano erupt. There's no way to protect myself. Nowhere to run. I can only stand here and burn. She screams loud enough that I wince. The only saving grace, the only positive thing I can think of is that we're the only ones in this inn. Beau and Mateo are somewhere in the building. Marjorie mentioned she sleeps on-site, but that's it. No other guests to complain about the child shrieking every word.

I kneel on the marble floor. The movement sets off a thousand aches in my body, which hasn't fully recovered from the fire. "I can see that you're upset. Let's take a deep breath. We don't have to take a bath right now. Let me ask if there are any other bathrooms we can use."

"There aren't," she says, her eyes wild. "There aren't. There aren't."

"Paige. Sweetheart. Let's go sit on the bed together." It's clear a bath isn't happening at the moment, and my concern right now is helping her calm down.

Except she's approaching panic, her wide gaze darting around the room, her little nostrils flaring as she pants. Fight or flight. "I don't want to sit on the bed. I don't want to take a bath. I don't want to do anything, anything, *anything.*"

The last words crescendo to a pitch that makes me flinch.

It's like I'm reflecting her own feelings, because panic rises in me. Logically I know that I'm safe here on this bathroom floor, but faced with her anxiety and the lingering fear from the fire, it doesn't feel that way. "Paige." My voice cracks, pleading. "Please."

She's beyond caring. "You can't make me. You're not my mom. You're not my dad. You're a stranger. You don't even belong here."

The words steal my air. They vacuum it right out of my lungs, leaving me gasping. Tears sting my eyes. I know, I *know* she's only saying it to lash out. It was a common enough refrain at the group and foster homes. It's not personal; it only feels that way. There's a squeeze in my chest. Hard enough that I bow my head before I can think of something to say.

Bang. The door from the bedroom slams open. Beau stands there, a dark expression on his handsome face. "Paige Louise Rochester, apologize right now."

She turns a mutinous face toward him. "*No.*"

I stand up, trying to head off disaster. Beau Rochester is stubborn and fierce, the strength of his will surpassed only by that of his niece. If they go head-to-head, I'm afraid that neither will be left standing. "She doesn't have to apologize. I'm fine. Really."

"Her behavior is completely out of line. Unacceptable."

Paige's lower lip wobbles, and I hold my breath. If she breaks down crying, I'm definitely going to start crying, too. All three of us still smell like disinfectant from the hospital. Bandages pull my skin every time I move. All I want is a hot bath and a long night's sleep. I've reached the end of my tether, and my breath feels shaky. *Don't cry, sweetheart. Don't cry.*

Paige doesn't cry. She screams.

CHAPTER SIX

Beau Rochester

DAMN MATEO. MAYBE it's completely a coincidence that he put my room next to Jane's, but I doubt it. The man knows it will drive me insane.

I should be on a different floor from her. It's too easy to pretend that we're back at the house before the fire. Too easy to imagine cornering her in the hallway. Each suite contains a sitting area overlooking the ocean. I recline on a floral armchair that feels too small, too fragile for my size, watching the endless horizon.

There's a gentle hum of voices, of feet on the hardwood floor. The whole inn has whispered ever since Paige's tantrum, afraid of waking the beast again. She cried herself to a shuddery sleep. I watched as Jane rocked her small body. Somehow they ended up curled against the baseboards in a corner. Begging. Ordering. Bargaining. We tried everything to get Paige to stop, but in the end it was the cradle of Jane's arms that worked.

Thank God for room service. And peanut butter and jelly sandwiches, which Paige ate even though the peanut butter was the crunchy kind. Then she fell into a deep, exhausted slumber on top of the coverlet. No bath today. We'll have to face it again tomorrow, but we'll all be calmer.

Sometimes the wisest course in a battle is retreat.

Water murmurs through the pipes. I fight the images that come to my head—Jane reclining in the copper clawfoot tub, water sluicing over her gorgeous skin. A wide faucet spills into the tub. There's an attachment you can hold instead. I imagine her holding it between her legs, the spray massaging her clit, her thighs shaking as she comes.

Christ. Now I'm hard.

Sex. It won't happen again. Brilliant idea, Rochester.

I know I should stay away from her, but it's hard to remember the reasons when I'm aching in my boxer briefs. The sun folds down, crouching beneath the water, only an eerie purple glow spreading out over the surface. This is what tourists come here for. This is why they rent this room, for this view of a beautiful sunset. My mind knows this. It's only my baser instincts that see it as sinister. This is the bay that claimed my brother's life. This is the water that beat against the cliffside, futile, uncaring, even as we almost burned.

There's a knock at the door. I remain still for a moment, hoping she'll go away. It's her. Of course it's her. The person I most long to see. The person I hunger for. The person I can barely stand to be around. Resentment rises, that she would come to me. Along with unholy anticipation.

The moment spins out, and I imagine her waiting, waiting, waiting.

How long will she wait?

Her feet are probably bare on the cold hardwood floor. Her arms crossed in a useless attempt at comfort. Her nipples are probably pebbles beneath her clothes.

I stand and cross the room. Open the door.

My imagination might have conjured her, except for her expression. It's reserved. Wary. And exhausted. She looks as reluctant to see me as I feel toward her. I can't help but look at her body in these new clothes, the way the pale pink shirt molds to her breasts, the way the black stretchy pants hug her thighs. Her dark hair falls around her face, tumbling over her shoulders.

I didn't think you'd be this angry, she said in the hospital. Anger is too simple a word for what I'm feeling. Fear and lust and possession. It's a form of madness, really. I can't let her have this much control over me, but even as I think the words, I'm worried it's too late.

"Yes?" I say, my voice low in warning.

There's an internal struggle. The arguments darken her eyes. Then she stands straighter. "I need to speak with you."

"Paige?"

"She's fine. Asleep."

"Then this can wait until morning." *When we won't be alone. When you won't look so small and tired and fragile.* Christ, why can't I stop looking at her body?

She's in a cotton shirt and yoga pants. Not the most alluring clothing. I've taken women to galas and then stripped them afterwards. I've dated a Victoria's Secret model, but I've never been more tempted than right now.

She smells faintly of the sweet orange soap that rests on the bathroom counters. I want to trail the damp strands of her hair over my chest and abs. I want to breathe along every plane of her skin, following the shadows to her sex. Want to lick, lick, lick until I draw her arousal, replacing the soap scent with her own.

"It can't wait," she says. "I need to talk to you without Paige around."

My stomach sinks. She would need to speak to me alone if she were going to quit. I step back so that she can come inside. Only when she's standing in my space, the door closing us in, the heat of her body a siren call do I realize I could have led her downstairs. The king-sized bed looms. It beckons. I can taste the phantom salt-sweet of her on my tongue.

I clear my throat. "Have a seat, then."

She ignores the two armchairs by the bay window and instead sits on a small padded stool by the dresser. One foot steps on the other. Nervous. She's nervous. I head to the minibar. Something tells me I'm going to need a stiff drink for this conversation.

"I need to ask you about the fire," she says.

Definitely vodka. I pull out a tiny bottle, twist off the cap, and drink it down in a fiery shot. "You want anything?" I ask her, reaching for a pop to wash it down.

"Did someone set that fire?"

"I told you not to listen to Causey."

"Because he's wrong? Or because you don't like what he's saying?"

She's too damned smart. I face her with the full force of my will. Powerful men have backed down across a boardroom, but she doesn't appear cowed. "Because he's full of shit."

"He told me that you went to school together."

"Which is how I know he's full of shit. He was the kind of kid who'd steal someone's lunch money and then kick them just to prove they could."

She fidgets. "A bully."

"Yes."

"We had bullies in the group homes. It was always good to go in pairs."

"That would have worked in my school, too. Except Joe was friends with my brother."

Her eyes widen, dark and bottomless. "Your brother let him do it?"

"My brother helped."

"How could he?"

My leg throbs, an echo of pain from long ago. "I don't want your sympathy, sweetheart. They stopped messing with me when I stopped caring about how hurt I got—no matter what they did, I got up. I went after them for so hard and so long

59

that they had to move on to easier prey."

"I hate that that happened to you."

My head shakes. How the hell does she have empathy for anyone else? I know what happened to her. Losing both her parents was bad enough. The abuse she endured in the foster care system is fucking unbearable. "I'm not going to win the competition for worst childhood."

"It's not a competition."

"Besides, whatever happened before, I'm over it."

She mutters something under her breath.

I should ignore it. "What?"

"I said you're full of shit."

A surprised bark of laughter. How am I supposed to resist her? How am I supposed to resist her when she's strong and fragile, smart and delicate? She calls me on my shit even while uncertainty shimmers in her midnight eyes. "Is that so?"

"Maybe you're over Joe Causey, but not your brother. You moved back to Maine to take care of his child. You've been living in his house. And now you're telling me that your rivalry with him included violence and bullying?"

"You can't hold a grudge against a dead man."

A sad smile flickers across her lips. "Can't

you? I still hold a grudge against my father. Oh, don't get me wrong. I loved him more than anything, but I don't know if I can ever forgive him for abandoning me."

My heart clenches. "Jane."

She stands, her movements jerky and fast. Agitated. She's agitated, and she paces across the small room. "I didn't come here to talk about my feelings."

"Now you're the one full of shit."

That earns me a hard look. She'll be formidable, this woman. She already is. "Regardless of whether Joe Causey is a good person or not, he said the fire chief thinks it's arson."

"The investigation is ongoing."

"You sound like some kind of PR spokesperson. Is it true?"

Christ. I was hoping to avoid a direct question. "The fire chief hasn't ruled out arson."

"So that means yes. Someone was at the house. Someone set the fire."

"We don't know that."

"You think so. I can see it in your eyes."

That makes me look away. The sun has fallen below the horizon, leaving only an inky black ocean in its wake. The only light in here comes from a small lamp, its shade gauzy and dreamlike.

"I didn't want you to worry."

"That's why you keep things from Paige. She's a *child*. I'm not."

Then I have to look at her, her earnest eyes and tense mouth, her body clad in casual clothes picked out by Mateo. Fuck me for being jealous that he got to choose what she wore. "Of course you're not a child. You think I don't know that? You're a beautiful, smart, desirable woman, and I'm having a hell of a time keeping my hands off you."

Her cheeks darken. "I deserve to know what's going on."

"Maybe that's true," I concede. "That doesn't stop me from wanting to protect you. To shield you from the ugliness of the world. Not because you can't handle it. Because you shouldn't have to."

She laughs so low and husky my cock takes notice. "This is your idea of ending things between us?"

I let out a growl. "You're the one knocking on my door at midnight. You're the one not wearing a bra. You're the one looking so damned tempting I can barely stand it."

"The bras he got me don't fit," she says, her cheeks darkening.

"Hell," I breathe, fighting desire. There's no willpower left. I cross the room in two long strides. Her eyes widen. That's the only chance she has to say no. She doesn't take it. My palms grasp her face, and then I'm kissing her. Consuming her. I'm muttering against her lips. "What am I supposed to tell you? That someone set a fire while I was fucking you? That I failed to protect you, failed to protect Paige, when you both needed me most?"

She pulls back, most likely to tell me that it's not my fault. That's the kind of thing Jane Mendoza would say. She's so quick to forgive a bastard like me. That's the only reason I'm allowed to touch her, to shove my hands underneath the soft T-shirt to her bare waist, to slide my hands up. My thumbs brush the underside of her breasts, and she moans.

"Damn right they didn't fit," I say, cupping her in my hand. "He doesn't know how they feel, the softness of them, the weight of them. He's never done this."

I bend my head and kiss her nipple. It hardens against my lips. The temptation is unholy. I lap at her, and she shivers in my arms. Moonlight casts a pale glow on her skin. I trace the letters on the plush slope of her breast. *Sorry. Sorry. Sorry.*

Her eyes are mournful. "Beau."

I suckle her again, until her eyes fall shut. I swirl her hard nub with my tongue. God, she tastes delicious. Woman and warmth. Salt and sea. I want to swallow her whole.

"Mr. Rochester."

The formality stops me in my tracks. It's like she dumped a bucket of cold water over me. I straighten and pull back. "Did I hurt you?"

"Yes," she whispers.

"Christ." I run my hands over her breasts, down her flat stomach. I'm looking for something. A cut, a bruise. Something left over from the fire that I touched. "Where?"

She takes my hand between both of hers. It makes me look fairly giant, my heavy fist encased in her small, delicate fingers. My palm lands on her chest. Her heart thumps beneath her sternum. "Here," she whispers. "You hurt me here."

It's not that you aren't beautiful. You are.

I told her I loved her in the fire. Then I tried to let her down easy in the hospital. There's no rhyme to it. No reason. The world can't reorder itself to make this relationship work. The boss and the nanny? No. It's wrong, but my body doesn't care. My heart sure as hell doesn't care either. I want her any way I can have her—secret, forbidden, taboo.

What I want doesn't matter.

Not if Paige might be in danger. Jane might be in danger, too. "I'm sorry," I say, but it's not a true apology. I'm not taking back my refusal. I'm affirming it. I can't be with her, not while there's still someone out there trying to hurt us. It's small and it's broken, this family—but it's mine.

CHAPTER SEVEN

Jane Mendoza

IT'S ALREADY BRIGHT outside when I wake up. There's a heavy feeling of exhaustion leftover from the fire like Dr. Gupta said there would be. But I have a job to do. A child to take care of. So I shower gingerly and head downstairs.

Beau's already gone from the Lighthouse Inn.

Visiting the house, Marjorie tells me.

Mateo's also gone, doing business, whatever that means.

It's only me and Paige and a breakfast spread on the sideboard that could feed an army.

There are large sticky cinnamon buns and eggs Benedict. Thick slices of bacon. Home fries. My stomach growls as I pile a plate high, reminding me that we haven't actually eaten much since the fire.

Paige crumbles a blueberry streusel muffin

into pieces. I can tell from the pile that she hasn't eaten much, but I don't want to pressure her.

"Do you want something else to eat? The fruit salad looks good."

She shakes her head. "No, thank you."

The small, polite tone makes my heart squeeze. Where is the wild, defiant girl I learned to care for in the house? She's hiding somewhere in those blue eyes. "I'll ask if she can make oatmeal tomorrow. Like you usually have for breakfast."

A shrug. I've never seen her this quiet. This withdrawn.

I almost prefer the screaming tantrum to this quiet version.

Of course she looks different, too, wearing a ruffled sky blue shirt with botanical drawings of flowers on it and a pair of skinny jeans. New clothes stock our wardrobes, but there is nothing in black tulle, nothing with Monopoly figures on it.

Beau left an envelope with my name scrawled across it. *Jane.* I've never seen his handwriting before. It's strong and messy, much like the man who wrote it. My cheeks turn warm. Inside there's a black AMEX with my name on it and a Post-it telling me to get whatever we need.

So I sit down at the small business corner with its fancy MacBook and start shopping. Cute T-shirts that say *I own the block* and *Go directly to jail, do not pass go* will not really fix her shock and trauma from the fire, but it's all I can do right now. I spend $500 on cute Monopoly-themed clothes from Etsy that are definitely not licensed.

Of course it's not only the clothes she loves. It's the game itself.

That becomes a problem, because there are many kinds of Monopoly. That's something I figure out pretty quickly. Paige doesn't want Maine-opoly or Ultimate Banking Edition or even a solid wood luxury version that costs $500.

"It's not the same," she says, her expression horrified that I'd even suggest such a thing.

She doesn't want the digital Nintendo version for Switch, either.

Unfortunately they don't make the very specific version of Monopoly anymore. It's one of the classic lines, the regular Monopoly, basically, but not the Updated and Improved version that retails at Target and toy stores right now.

So I browse eBay trying to find the right combination of keywords that will give me the exact board game Paige loves to replace the one that burned.

Though nothing will really fix the fact that her Vermont Avenue had a bent corner. Or that her Chance card deck had been chewed by the kitten. Or that this was the same set passed down from her father, Rhys Rochester, who had played the game as a child.

It's an heirloom, and it's gone.

Beau walks into the room while I'm busy scrolling through eBay and a million Facebook Shopping posts. I tense, because I'm not sure who he is to me now. I'm not sure what he expects from me now. Not sex, that much is clear.

But I don't know how to go from lover to stranger.

Is he Beau or is he Mr. Rochester?

Whatever I call him, he's a man I care about far more than I should.

He said he loved me when the house was burning, but maybe he didn't mean it. Maybe it's something he said in the heat of the moment. Men say *I love you* during sex. It could be that believing you're going to die is the same way—temporary emotion powered by adrenaline. But I know the truth. He did mean it.

You said you love me, I told him.

He hadn't denied it. *It doesn't matter. My love is dangerous.*

He looks windblown and severe, though considerably less intimidating when Kitten trails in after him, looking windblown as well. "Kitten," I whisper, and she does a hopping jump over to me. I press my face into her supersoft fur and breathe in her scent. Though it's tinged with something medicinal. "Did the vet give her a clean bill of health?"

"Yes," he says softly, his dark eyes stormy.

"Then what's wrong?"

He glances where Paige sleeps on the window seat across from me.

There's no slip in his expression. A stranger might not see the worry, the fear, the deep hope he has for her emotional recovery, but I can. A stranger might not see the pain that pulls at him, stabs at him, the pain in his leg that he seems determined to hide. He didn't hide it after the fall. He used his crutches even as he cursed at them. It's only now, after the fire, as if he thinks he brought the disaster down on us with his own fragile humanity.

Paige has been napping most of the afternoon. That's normal, according to my preliminary Google searches about recovering from trauma. The body needs sleep to heal. So does the brain, it says. But I wonder if we need to do something for her. A therapist, maybe. I'm not sure what Beau will think about that.

He comes to stand close, murmuring low so as not to wake her. "The fire chief let me come in and take some things from the scene, so I looked through the wreckage. Nothing much was salvageable, but I boxed up what I could find. I stacked it in the back."

"What did he say?"

"He didn't say anything yet. They gathered evidence, but he hasn't made his determination yet. I'm going to meet him in a couple days and get his final ruling when he releases the scene."

Unease clenches my stomach. I want a ruling, because it will put my mind at ease. But what if the ruling isn't what I want? "I'll see if any of her stuff is in there. We can wash out the smoke."

"Hell, buy her all new shit. Make it fucking expensive." Another glance to the sleeping child. And a sigh. "But yeah, she would rather have her old clothes."

"Maybe I would rather have my old clothes, too."

He gives me a hard look. Everything I wore before was from Walmart or Goodwill, threadbare or secondhand, except what he gave me. "What did you lose?"

I shake my head. "It's nothing."

"It's something." The gravity of him pulls me closer. "Tell me, Jane."

"It was a photo. I kept it at the bottom of my suitcase. Before that, I'd get a garbage bag to carry my things. So it was creased and folded and spilled on, but it was the only picture I had." Tears gather, hot and sharp. I don't want to cry. Definitely not in front of Beau, but they spill over anyway. It was the only picture I had, with his illegible handwriting scrawled on the back. The only semblance of a family heirloom that existed in my life. Gone.

"I'll find it," he says, his teeth gritted.

"Don't." The word comes out like an order. "Don't make promises you can't keep."

I'm talking about more than an old, bent photograph. I'm talking about us. About this strange purgatory we're living since the fire. He understands. The knowledge sits in his dark eyes. "I'm not lying to you, Jane."

"You're not telling me the whole truth, either."

He looks away. It's an admission. A refusal. My heart squeezes, but then he looks back at me and pins me with a stare. "I would tell you everything if I didn't think you'd run for the hills."

"Is that supposed to be comforting?"

A ghost of a smile. "Not really."

I glance at Paige, because it's easier to talk about her. It's easier to use her as a wedge between us. Ironic, because she's also the glue keeping us together. "I'll have to check the boxes for the game. There's nothing that's an exact match online. So far she shakes her head at everything I show her."

"There's no way the game made it through the fire. I'll get in touch with Hasbro and see if they have something in a warehouse somewhere. Or at least a line to a collector."

A soft laugh, which makes me cough. My eyes sting as I force it to be as quiet as possible. "Sometimes you seem almost normal. And then other times, you're…"

His lips quirk. "I'm what?"

"Rich."

He frowns as if I said something wrong, though it can hardly be a surprise that he's wealthy. "Clothes. Board games. That's what money is good for. It doesn't help with the important things."

"Like what?" I ask, my tone challenging.

A glance at Paige. He pitches his voice lower.

"Like keeping her safe."

Worry runs through my veins. "What does that mean?"

"We're in a new place. You know how she likes to hide. We'll have to keep a close eye on her. That's all I mean." He looks sincere. He sounds sincere.

I swallow hard. "Beau, did someone set that fire?"

"I told you Causey is a bastard. Don't let him get into your head."

"Then what started it?"

"They don't know yet, and there's no point assuming the worst. There are a million options in an old house. Faulty wiring and materials that aren't up to code."

"Or someone put the chemicals there to start a fire." My heart thumps heavy with the possibility. It's been in my head since Detective Joe Causey questioned me.

"We were the only ones in the house."

I shiver. "That we know of."

"It was the middle of the night. We stood outside the house and didn't see anyone standing around holding a gasoline can or lighting a match."

"Right," I say, my throat dry. Except it was

pitch black that night. It's terrifying to think there might have been someone in the trees watching us. Waiting to see if we'd die in the fire or make it out alive. Maybe wanting to finish us off, if the fire truck hadn't arrived in time.

"You're cold," he says, pulling me up from the sofa. His arms wrap around me, but I don't feel their warmth. I'm not cold, precisely. I'm scared. What kind of crazy person sets a house on fire?

"What are we going to do?" I whisper.

"We're going to hire a construction company. Rebuild. Restore. Move back in. I'm paying enough that they'll drop their other jobs to work on mine."

Then we'll know how it happened, but how will we find the person who did it? I suppose that's a question for the cops, but I learned early not to trust the cops. Or teachers. Or nurses. They have too much power. And children have too little. I glance at Paige, anxious for her.

"She's fine," Beau says, reading my mind. "I don't want her to worry. I don't want you to worry either, but you need to keep your guard up. In case…"

"In case what?" *In case whoever set the fire tries again.* The words hang between us. I wish they were mocking, his dark eyes. Taunting. It would make this a joke, instead of serious.

He looks grave as the night. "In case Detective Causey comes around."

"He already questioned me."

A grim smile. "I have no doubt he'll be back. And based on the way he tried to ambush Paige when I left the hospital, he'll probably try to catch you alone, too."

"I won't let him get near Paige." The detective made me uncomfortable. I don't know whether it's my old fear of authority or something deeper. Regardless, I'm not going to let him question Paige. "Why's he so suspicious? Even if someone did set the fire, it seems like he should be looking at other people. Not just us."

Beau gives a half shrug. "It's in his nature."

I glance away, a little nervous. A little scared. "I'll protect her."

"I trust you to protect Paige, but I need you to do more than that. I need you to protect yourself."

A shiver runs down my spine. "Do you think he's dangerous?"

"I think I don't trust anyone until we know what happened that night." That only raises more questions. More concerns. Every single thing I learn about Beau Rochester only pulls me deeper into murky water. He must see it in my face, because he gives a short shake. "Anyway, Paige is resting. You should be resting, too."

"No, I'm fine."

A dark look. "That wasn't a suggestion. It was an order."

I remember Mrs. Fairfax's words. *I see the way you look at him. And more importantly, I see the way he looks at you.* He's looking at me now, his gaze a dark pool of secrets. What does he really think about me? What does he want from me?

The same thing I want from him, possibly.

Or nothing at all.

I love you, damn you. He said the words to me when we were inside the burning house. And the worst part is, he meant them. He told me his love is dangerous, but he's wrong. His love didn't start that fire. His love didn't kill Emily Rochester.

"A boss couldn't tell me to rest," I tell him, almost gentle in my rebuff. "Only a lover could do that. And you've already made it clear that you won't be mine. Your love is dangerous, remember? Your love starts fires and wars. Your love is a category five hurricane."

His gaze turns sharp. "This isn't a game."

My cheeks heat. He's going to break my heart. "Even if you don't want me, you can't go on believing this. Forget about me. Paige needs you."

At the sound of her murmured name, she rustles. There's a murmur, and then her eyes flutter. She's coming awake. Beau looks at her, and in his dark eyes, I see the love he has for her. The fear he has for her, because he believes it. *My love is dangerous.*

He walks out of the room before Paige stretches and sits up. I feel rejected all over again—the same way I felt in the hospital bed. Embarrassed and small. Most of all, alone. Except I have a small child with me now, one with rumpled hair and sleepy eyes. She needs me.

CHAPTER EIGHT

Jane Mendoza

I FEEL SLIGHTLY more normal the next day. More like I've been hit with a regular hammer instead of a sledgehammer. The bruises on my body from falling debris turn an ugly green.

"More syrup than that," Paige says.

She's sitting at the kitchen island, her gaze glued to the mini pitcher in my hand. Amber maple syrup spills down onto the stack of pancakes I've made her. Marjorie took the morning off—an appointment, she said—so it's just us in the kitchen. "More than that."

"Your pancakes are going to float away."

"Then make them float," she says, expression serious.

I tiptoe right up to the edge of floating the pancakes on the sturdy china Marjorie uses, then stop pouring it with a laugh. "Let's save a little bit for me."

"Is it all gone?" Beau asks from the doorway. He has a stack of paper in his hands. I don't know how he could be reading it, what with all the pacing he's doing. He keeps looping back to the kitchen, pausing in the doorway, and going away again.

"Not quite." I cut my glance toward the cupboard. Marjorie is too competent of a bed-and-breakfast owner to actually run out of syrup. "But we might be getting close if Paige needs her pancakes to sail away on a syrup ocean."

She grins at me through a mouthful of pancakes. My heart squeezes. She's been so pale and quiet and unsettled since the fire, but this morning she seems like she's starting to get used to it. Maybe we all are. As soon as I think it, I become aware of my clothes again. Thick, expensive fabric, and soft. Not the sturdy cotton that most hand-me-downs are made out of.

From the outside, no one would be able to tell that I don't really belong here with Beau and Paige. All they'd see, if they looked in the window, is a woman and a little girl making breakfast, and a man hovering around like a moth drawn in to a flame again and again. They'd probably see a little family.

There's nobody out there, but when I turn back to flip the pancakes I check the window. Nothing but a fresh, clean day. Warm out already. Buttery sunlight. Plants tentatively starting to bloom. It's unseasonably warm, according to Marjorie. Warm enough that people are swimming in the ocean. Not me. I'll go to the beach with Paige, but we're sticking to sandcastles away from the cold water's edge.

Beau leans against the doorframe and scans the papers he's brought with them.

"Do you want any pancakes?" Paige cranes her neck to look at him.

His eyes come up from the papers to meet hers, and then they move to mine. My pulse ticks up. Is that longing in his eyes? Does Beau Rochester want to be invited to sit down to breakfast with us? That's what would happen in that picture-perfect family. I would serve them pancakes at the kitchen island. He'd sit there next to Paige and tease her about the lake's worth of syrup on her plate. I would laugh. We would be happy.

Beau blinks like he's clearing a similar vision from his mind. "I'm all right. Thanks, sweetheart."

Paige screws up her lips in a pout, but it disappears just as quickly. Beau's footsteps travel up the stairs to the second floor. A door closes with a soft *click* just as the back door opens.

Mateo steps in from the outside, bathed in golden morning light, looking exactly like an ultra-hot movie star.

Because he is an ultra-hot movie star.

Right now, he looks the part. A towel is slung low on his hips, held in place with one of his fists, and his dark hair glistens. He runs a hand through it, tousling it just so, and he flashes me a smile that looks as expensive as his carved abs.

His abs.

Which are on display. Fully. If the towel moved another inch…

"Morning, Jane. Hi, Paige."

I remember I'm looking at a human being and not a movie poster and almost drop the spatula into the frying pan. My face heats. It's not that I'm attracted to Mateo. He's just attractive. It's a natural reaction in the presence of a gorgeous man like he is. "Morning, Mateo. How was your swim?"

"Bracing," he answers. He hasn't dried himself off all the way, despite the towel. Water droplets still cling to his shoulders and the ridges of his abs. I need to stop looking at them immediately.

"It clears my head to wake up that way. Straight from bed to the ocean."

"Does it? I'd freeze, I think."

"You don't freeze if your body stays moving. Besides, the ocean is warmer than it looks this time of year. Once you're in it's not so bad."

"Yeah, but those first few steps are enough to make a girl change her mind."

"It's always hardest below the waist," Mateo says.

"What is?" Beau asks from the doorway. "Think about your answer before you say it, Mateo."

✧　✧　✧

Beau Rochester

I CAME BACK down here for some goddamn pancakes, and what do I find but Mateo half-naked in the kitchen, flirting his ass off.

With Jane. My Jane.

And I know she's not mine. I know she might never be. But fuck if I'll let this happen under the roof of this inn. Fuck if I'll let this happen while I'm in the same house.

Jane blushes scarlet. "Did you decide on pancakes after all?"

"Yes." I stride into the kitchen, toss the folder

on the other side of the island, and take the seat next to Paige. "If you're still making them. Or maybe you want some."

She bites her lip. "I do, but I'll make them at the same time as yours."

"Beau," says Mateo. His words mean, *Calm the fuck down.*

"What about you?" I look him in the eye and try to get this bristling, snapping feeling under control. I don't like the way he looked at Jane. I don't like the way he spoke to her. And I have no right to say a damn thing. "Are you here to eat pancakes?"

"Yeah," says Paige. "Are you?"

He's standing there in a towel, and I'm obviously pissed and trying to hide it. The whole thing is so ridiculous I could laugh. Except what I want to do is pin Jane to the counter and kiss her in front of him so it's clear who she should belong to.

"Of course," says Mateo. "As long as it's fine with everybody."

"By all means." I say it too loud, and Jane looks between Mateo and me. It's like she can't decide whether to smile or frown. I can't decide whether this is the most awkward moment of my life or just par for the course.

Mateo glances over the scene in front of him. Paige, with her fork in her fist. Me, with both hands on the table, trying not to punch him. "Let me go change, and I'll be back for pancakes."

"Great."

He leaves, and the tension decreases in the room. Jane turns back to the stove and flips three more pancakes onto a plate. She slides it in front of me. "Are you okay?"

"Yes. Everything's great. The house burned down and Mateo's walking around here naked."

"He had a towel on."

"He was flirting with you wearing it." Paige is absorbed in her pancakes, cutting them up into tiny pieces and dunking them farther into the syrup, humming a song under her breath.

"And?" Jane arches an eyebrow, her cheeks turning pink. "It doesn't mean anything. That's how how he is. And besides, he's single."

"He's always single. He's always just single enough to go after the nearest available woman."

Her dark gaze dares me to say it. I'm frozen with my fork halfway to the pancakes. I want my mouth on hers. I want her body against mine. I don't want anything else.

"That would be me," she says. Her shyness is chipping away bit by bit. I can't help but be proud of her, even though it breaks my sense of control. "The nearest available woman."

"You think you're available for him?"

"I don't know. You tell me, Mr. Rochester."

Paige lifts a bite of pancake on her fork and holds it up to the light. Ten more seconds of Jane looking at me this way and I'll end this, here and now, damn the consequences. I'll tell her the truth, which is that she's mine, and Mateo Garza, the Oscar-award-winning actor and national heartthrob, in a goddamn towel will never change that. Even if I'm wrong for her. My love is dangerous, but it's fucking real.

"Don't think for an instant, Jane, that you're—"

"I'm back," Mateo announces, having pulled a T-shirt on without drying off. The web fabric molds to his muscles. He slides onto the stool next to mine.

I force myself to relax. This tension wasn't between him and Paige. It's between the two of us. That's what I feel in this room.

"How are the pancakes?" he asks.

I swallow the rest of the sentence. "Delicious," I tell him, keeping my gaze on Jane. "Tastes better than anything I've ever had."

CHAPTER NINE

Beau Rochester

THE OCEAN ROLLS forward, forward, forward, ever moving over the shore but never quite reaching it. Moonlight winks across the surface. I'm sitting in the armchair again—waiting for Jane, if I'm honest. I heard the sounds of water in the pipes. Footsteps on the floorboard.

And then the entire inn quieted.

An hour passed.

Then two.

She's not coming to visit me again, not to berate me and certainly, certainly not to have sex with me. I only have myself to blame, but it doesn't stop the frustration. Now I have to imagine her knocking on Mateo's door instead. It doesn't make my cock any less hard. It's throbbing, hungry, wanting inside a certain woman only a few yards away.

The ocean provides the rhythmic soundtrack to my desire.

Perhaps I drift to sleep. I'm woken by the sound of a cry from the hallway. My joints have stiffened in the cool night air, my leg screams in protest, but I stride across the room. There's only one thought: *Paige.* She had nightmares when her parents died.

Maybe the fire started them up again.

The hallway is a startling black, like plunging into the ocean. No windows. No moonlight. I move by sense and feel. I find the paneled wood grain of her door beneath my palm. I fumble along the wallpaper until I reach the switch.

The lamp casts a yellow glow across the room.

A small form sleeps beneath the covers, very still. I step closer. Pale lashes rest against her cheek. Blonde curls sprawl across her pillow. A small hand lies half-open, unguarded in this moment. I feel a pang of protectiveness. A certainty that I would throw myself in front of a train for this child. That I would pull down the moon if she needed it.

She looks sweet, but also deeply asleep. Peaceful, even.

Did her nightmare end? Did I imagine it?

Kitten looks up from her slumber, cat eyes

glowing yellow in the dark. She's tucked against Paige's side. The kitten looks drowsy, too. As if I'm the one who disturbed her. She would already be awake if Paige had been tossing and turning.

The cry comes again, this time louder and clearer. It wasn't coming from this room at all. It's from the room next door, and through the wall, I can feel the urgency. The fear. I move out of the room, careful to turn the light off and slide the door closed. *Quiet, quiet.*

I pause right outside Jane's door, wondering whether I should knock, debating the appropriateness of going inside. Of course there is no debate. It's not appropriate. I'm her boss. I have no right to enter her bedroom.

The knob turns in my hand. I push open the door, coming face-to-face with pitch black. Someone's closed the curtains in this room. Moonlight barely penetrates the fabric. This time I don't bother with the light. That's not what she needs.

Instead I move across the room, letting my eyes adjust to the moonlight.

Shadows drape across the large bed. She looks larger than Paige but not by much. She's still small and vulnerable. Jane brings out the protective instinct in me, though it's very different with this grown woman. It feels darker. Possessive. Sexual. Except, of course, I can't have sex with her. For her own sake. For mine. For the safety of this small, dysfunctional family.

A soft cry comes from the bed, and I drop a knee onto the mattress. It rolls her toward me. I grasp her arm and shake.

She thrashes in the bed, fighting the sheets, fighting me. Fighting invisible demons.

"Jane," I say, shaking her harder. "Wake up."

A fist lands on my chest. My jaw. I grunt as she manages to knee me in the stomach.

I catch her hands and pin them to the bed. "Goddamn it, wake up."

A gasp. Then she opens her eyes wide. I can see the whites in the inky dark, the stark fear that vibrates through her body. I stare at her, holding her, willing her to know she's safe. Relief crashes over her in a tidal wave. Her eyes flutter closed. Her body goes boneless in my arms. "Beau," she says, her voice hoarse and intimate. It's the sound of a woman who's just woken up in the same bed. The sound of a woman with her lover.

My cock hardens. The sweet sleepy scent of her, the warm softness—all of it makes hunger tighten in my body. I want to kiss every dark thought. I want to fuck away her nightmares. I settle for pulling back with a businesslike nod. "You were having a bad dream."

She reaches for me. Her hand pauses in the air, halted by every barrier between us. She's so much younger than me. Far too innocent for the images flashing through my mind. She wants comfort, not sex, but she's too naive to know the difference.

Maybe I'm naive, too.

A heavy beat runs through my veins. *Take her. Mark her. Make her mine.* I've walked away from million dollar deals, but it feels impossible to walk away from her. She's a siren. I'll throw myself against the jagged cliffs, turning the ocean pink with my blood.

Her hand hovers in the air. Indecision. Uncertainty.

I'm holding my breath. Holding it as she reaches for me. Her knuckles brush my cheek. There's a faint rasp against the bristles. "I know you don't want to have sex," she says.

And I have to hold back the laugh. The hysterical laugh. The howl of denial. I don't want to have sex with her? It's the only thing I can think about. I need it more than I need air.

A breath whooshes out of her. "Can you hold me?"

Can I hold her without fucking her? I'm not sure. It's a request of purity, but there's nothing pure about my thoughts. *Walk away while you still can.* Too late for that. I press my face into her hand, breathing in the salt scent of her skin, pressing a kiss to the fluttery pulse at her wrist. How can I turn away from her when she needs something, anything?

This has nothing to do with Beau Rochester. That's what I tell myself. I'm a warm body. A temporary cure for the loneliness and the fear. So I slide beneath the floral coverlet. Her body curls into my arms as if she was made to be held by me.

I rest my chin on the top of her head, my eyes wide open in the dark. How the hell am I going to walk away? How can I live without holding her every second of every goddamn day?

"I'll hold you until you fall asleep," I mutter, knowing that I'll have to leave.

"Thank you," she whispers, her breath hot against my chest.

Dread unfurls in my stomach. This was how the fire started. I lost myself in her and let my guard down. If I gave in and touched her, or worse, slept the night with her in my arms, we'd be in danger again. Maybe not tonight or tomorrow night, but it would only be a matter of time.

When did I learn that love meant danger?

Before the fire. Before Paige's parents drowned. No, I learned it as a child, when I was getting my ass kicked behind the elementary school. When I coughed up my own tooth, when I fought so hard even Joe Causey, the bully two years older and a good fifty pounds heavier, backed down, my brother watching in dark fascination.

Jane moves in my arms, restless. She's seeking something. Comfort? Safety? My primitive brain thinks she's seeking pleasure, and I'm damned well ready to give it to her.

"What was your nightmare about?" I ask. It's a cruel question. A trick question, because there's nothing guaranteed to splash cold water on my lust more than hearing her fear.

"You," she whispers, and I go still in shock.

There's true tragedy in her past. Abuse and hardship. We barely made it out of a goddamn inferno, but it's not those things she dreams about. "Me?"

"You were angry at me."

Angry because she almost died in the fire. Angry because I couldn't save her. There's no air in my lungs. It feels like I've been punched in the stomach. It hurts worse than anything Joe Causey could ever do to me. "Sweetheart."

"I couldn't leave you."

A shudder runs through my body. "God, sweetheart. Of course you couldn't. It was too much to ask of you, living with that knowledge. And it was too much to ask of me, watching you burn. It was a goddamned unholy night, both of us ruined. Forgive me, forgive me."

"Yes," she says in a broken whisper. "Yes. Yes. Yes." She should be terrified of my guilt-drenched ramblings, but she seems to understand. She moves as if to get closer, though it hardly feels possible. She'll climb inside me. She'll burrow under my skin.

I hold her as tight as I did in the fire, my fingers probably leaving bruises. There are no flames. No falling ash. Only the bone-deep certainty that if I don't hold on, I'll lose her. "Let me," I tell her, running a hand over her hip and between her thighs. I'm breaking my own damn rule, but I don't care. "Let me make it better. I'll touch you until you cream on my palm, until you're slick and messy. I'll touch you until you forget all about the nightmare."

Her hips rock away from my questing hands. And then back. She's skittish, this woman, this goddess. I made her this way. I cup her sex in apology. In reassurance. I might be a coldhearted bastard, but her body trusts me. She's already wet. Was she slick when she dreamed about me? When she writhed in her nightmare? Did she know, even then, that I would kiss her better? I run my middle finger through the slickness. My cock flexes in my jeans, wanting that wetness, wanting this heat. *No.* This isn't about me. It's about Jane.

The pad of my middle finger makes circles around her clit. Once. Twice. Three times and she bucks her hips. She's so hungry for it. Maybe this is the medicine she needs. Not the orange pill bottles the hospital sent home. Not the butterfly bandages or the salve. She needs this pussy fucked—by my fingers, my tongue. My cock. Anything will work.

"Beau," she says, the word ending in a whine. "I need… I need…"

"Say it for me, sweetheart. Tell me what this little pussy needs."

Her hands grasp at me—my shirt, my hair. She's drowning in sensation, and I'm the current, dragging her to the bottom. "You," she breathes.

My breath hitches at the admission. There's only a small pause, a split second where I wonder what the hell I'm doing here, where I sail over the cliff, on my way down. Then I'm on top of her, around her, kissing her like this is the last chance I'll ever get. I push two fingers inside her sweet cunt. Her inner muscles pull me deeper, and I groan at the sweet sensation. I want to feel her around my cock, but I know I don't deserve that. Not yet.

I move down her body, spreading her legs wide. She squirms, sensing where I'm going, what I'm doing. I've tasted her before, but she was tipsy then. Now she's sober. And shy. It makes me harder, of course. Everything she does makes me harder. I'm determined to do this, to show her my apology this way. My palms push her thighs apart, revealing her to me—all dark, musky surrender. I press my face into her sex and nuzzle into her curls, reveling in the salt scent of her. God, she's delicious. Woman and desire. I find the slick, dark center of her. I slide my tongue from the bottom to the top, feeling her smoothness, her secret skin. At the top I lash her clit, the place I touched with my middle finger, I circle with my tongue. She moans.

Her hips rock in little desperate movements. I have no desire to rush her to the finish line. Not when my cock throbs against the sheets of the bed, leaking precum onto the sheets. I want to draw this out—for her pleasure and my pain.

I write her a message on her clit, the most sensitive place on her body with the most tactile part of mine, drawing each letter with a lash. *I LOVE YOU.*

And then I continue, *DAMN YOU.*

She's making little sobbing sounds by the end. I have to hold down her hips to keep her steady. Her body undulates against the mattress. She's damn near begging me to fuck her, and my cock wants to do it, but something holds me back. Guilt. Dread. Some sense that if I fuck her, if I sleep in her bed, we'll wake up in a raging fire again.

I attack her clit with focus, with the intensity I can't give her. I spell out the words I can't say, until she breaks apart in my arms, her cunt wet against my mouth, her desire sweet as I lick it up. She collapses on the bed, her body boneless. I move to lie down next to her. Yes, my cock hurts like a motherfucker. So does my leg, for that matter. It's pain that I've earned. Pain that I deserve. I'm not sure when my crimes started. Was it when I risked Jane's life in the fire? Or was it earlier, when I walked away from Emily when she needed me? I can't be what a woman needs. I'll only hurt her. It's inevitable.

She curves herself over my body, her legs straddling me, a goddess rising from the water, all bronze skin and dark hair, her hands uncertain on my cock. I grunt against the sudden pleasure, the urge to come right there and then. I watch from beneath slitted eyes as she lifts her body.

"Is this right?" she asks, breathless, fitting the head of my cock against her slick core.

If I were a better man, a good man, I'd take her hips in my hands. I'd fuck her from underneath, make this easy, but instead I watch her struggle. I relish each brush of her soft, clumsy fingers against my hardness. I enjoy the awkward angle of her body as she rides a man for the very first time. For a moment it seems like it won't happen, like we'll be poised on this precipice forever, the wrong angle, the slightest bite of pain—and then all at once she slides down. We're connected completely, effortlessly, her body completely enveloping mine, her hips resting on me.

"Oh," she says, her eyes wide with wonder.

"Yes," I grunt. "Like that."

There is no steady rhythm. She doesn't know it yet, and that hint of innocence makes my chest ache. I let her ride me in abrupt, eager starts. My cock doesn't know the difference. It just wants inside her. Inside her sweet heat. Her hands rest on my chest, taking strength from me. It's how I want her to be, always leaning on me, always needing me.

I put my thumb against her clit—lightly, lightly. Only enough that she can brush against me every time she rocks forward. Her breath catches. Now that she has the right incentive, she finds the rhythm, pushing her clit against my thumb, again and again, her smooth pearl against my callused pad, becoming slicker and slicker around my cock. Her eyes drift shut as she loses herself in pleasure, but I can't do the same. I can't close my eyes. I can't look away from the goddess that rides me, her breasts moving with erotic grace, her face gorgeous as she climaxes. Her pussy clamps down hard, dragging an orgasm from me, milking my cock as I shudder and ache beneath her.

CHAPTER TEN

Beau Rochester

J ANE MENDOZA IS one of those women who gets energy from thorough sex. Her eyes are wide open in the dark. And she's chatty. I find this fact about her incredibly hot. It makes me want to fuck her all over again just to find out what else she'll share.

Unfortunately she's actually quite tired. And she needs to rest. I'm not going to fuck her into a state of dehydrated exhaustion where she needs to go back to the hospital.

"You should sleep," I say, planting a kiss on her forehead.

"I don't want to."

I narrow my eyes. "Who's the nanny here?"

She stretches, her limbs long and sinuous in the moonlight, her skin the color of sand at night. "Seriously, I feel like I could run a marathon right now."

"And someday, I'll fuck you so good and so hard and so long, then send you out with a bottle of water, and we'll see if it works. But right now? You need to sleep."

"Wait." Her eyes look serious now. She shifts so we're facing one another. Her limbs move against mine beneath the sheets, her legs smooth against my rough hair, the soft rasp making my cock flex. I want her spread open beneath me.

Will I ever get enough of her?

It strikes me with both hunger and fear, that thought.

What if I'm always this desperate for a taste of her? What if I'm always this hard to get inside her? Every time I touch her, my need seems to grow. My feelings for Emily were overwhelming. Obsessive. And they nearly killed me. There's a real chance they killed her. What I feel for Jane is so much deeper, so much darker. What if we never make it out of the abyss?

"What?" I mutter, unable to look her in the eye, unable to pull away. I wrap her tightly in my arms, tight enough that I expect her to squirm or gasp for air. She does neither.

"You saw me dreaming."

"It was dark, but technically, yes."

"And you know my… secrets." Her voice goes low, but in the sultry way. In the scared way. As if she's thinking of that night of the fire, when she told me about how she lost her virginity. To the bastard who was supposed to take care of her.

"And now I want to track down someone and shoot them." I'm going to do it, actually. Not with a gun, though that sounds fun. Maybe with my bare fists. Or maybe I'll just crush him with money. They all sound like a fun time. I'm going to enjoy myself absolutely ruining that man. But she doesn't ever need to know about that.

Her lashes brush her cheeks. She doesn't want to look at me. Shy—even as her pussy's still wet and swollen from my cock. It's heartbreaking. "I want you to tell me something about you. Something other people don't know."

"Is this some kind of a game?"

"No, it's some kind of intimacy. So I don't feel so… naked."

"I like you naked," I say, looking down at her to prove the point. God, she's beautiful. Those small tits, just enough to touch and tweak her dark pink nipples. I want to come on them next time. I want so much more than that, but I'm afraid to freak her out. So I give her a very basic, very boring fact about me that no one actually knows. "I hate lobster."

"You hate lobsters?"

"No, I mean I hate them as animals, sure, but I specifically hate the taste. They're basically bottom feeders, so you're getting all the pollution in the ocean. Concentrated in a few ounces of meat. And you just slather it with butter so no one notices the taste of chemical runoff."

"But everyone loves lobster."

"Back when Maine was still a colony, only the poor ate lobster. Livestock ate lobster. Prisoners ate so much lobster that it was deemed cruel and unusual punishment."

"Okay, this doesn't count as intimacy."

"What? I've never told anyone that."

"Because it's random. Not because it's important to you."

I sigh. "I hate this game."

"It's not a game," she says, slapping my chest. "I told you. Intimacy."

"Fine. Fine. Here's something no one knows. And something that's important to me. I only wear boxer briefs. Boxers are too loose. Briefs are too tight. Boxer briefs are perfect."

"Oh my God," she says, exasperated.

"What?"

She sucks in a breath, as if gathering courage.

"Tell me about Emily."

I stop moving. Every muscle in my body goes still. Even my heart. "What about her?"

"I don't know. Anything. Tell me about her."

I thought I understood what it was like for Jane to share that story with me. It would be hard. She'd feel nervous, naturally. That was apparently a huge understatement.

Actually sharing hard shit feels like knives inside my stomach. I guess this is intimacy, cutting open your old scars to show people around inside them.

"She moved to town. I fell for her. Hard."

"She was beautiful?"

"She was everything I thought a woman should be, even though we were only seventeen at the time. Beautiful. Smart. She had this way of carrying herself that made everyone look twice." A rueful smile. "And maybe I liked her because she made me work for it. I went after her for all of senior year, but she wouldn't let me past second base."

Jane makes a face. "Not easy like me."

"Nothing about you is easy," I say on a sigh, my face against her stomach.

"You're just saying that because you want me to have sex with you again."

"Oh, you're definitely having sex with me again. But you're nothing like her. It was a game. She knew it was a game. We both did. Flirt with all the boys and see who wins a date."

"And you were the winner?"

"I thought I was. I felt like a winner. She was mine. My girlfriend. We were going steady. But she wanted more than a house on the water. More than a lobsterman's life. So I started building my business. The investors wanted me in LA where I could network with the right funding people, build a team of developers. I left her with my class ring on her finger."

"Like an engagement ring?"

"A promise ring, at the very least. I thought she'd wait for me. Or at least call if she got tired of waiting." It's a foolish thing, but I find myself touching her finger. Her fourth finger, where a ring would go.

She laces her hand in mine.

"I was cocky enough not to expect a Dear John letter at all, but I sure as hell didn't expect it to come from my brother. He called me to tell me they got engaged."

"Oh, Beau."

"It's not a sad story. Well, it was sad at the time. I was pissed. And then drunk. And then pissed again. But really it was just a natural culmination of what we'd been doing the whole time. Being shitheads who cared more about winning than anything else."

"Did you ever talk to her about it?"

"The business was already successful. After that happened, I pushed hard for a buyout. A big payday for everyone. I wanted the money, the success, to show her what she was missing. But then in the blink of an eye she was married to him, and it didn't fucking matter anymore."

"Of course it mattered. You loved her."

"Love. What a strange idea."

She puts a hand on my chest. Emotion. That's what she means. What's happening deep in my heart, in the bones and sinew of my body—but instead I feel only what's on the surface. The slight weight of her hand, the smoothness of her palm, how badly I want her to keep moving her arm down. "You loved her. And you loved Rhys. Otherwise it wouldn't have hurt when they betrayed you."

"Or maybe I just didn't like losing. Whatever the reason, I had more money than sense. I already knew Mateo. It was easy to fall into his crowd with money to throw around."

"And then suddenly you disappeared."

Her eyes are so dark and so wide. Luminous. I push a strand of hair out of her face. "The way you look at me... with so much trust. And kindness. It's only because you think I'm someone else. If you knew the real me, you'd look at me different."

An eye roll. "I could say the same thing about you."

Except she's wrong. I've already seen into the very core of her. The inherent goodness of her. This isn't a game to her. I should have known that. I should never have touched her. This hasn't been a game for her, and the worst part, it hasn't been a game for me either. "One day Emily showed up at my penthouse. I was drunk. And completely taken by surprise. She'd been arguing with Rhys, she said. They were getting a divorce."

Jane sucks in a breath. She can see where this is going.

"Yeah." I drop my head back on the pillow, feeling like a bastard for the millionth time. "I slept with her. It was stupid. And it was bad. And it was cheating."

"Because she wasn't really getting a divorce, was she?"

"No. I mean, maybe she thought about it, but it wasn't going to happen. Even as I was fucking her, she had to know that it was a revenge fuck. I wasn't going to marry my brother's ex. I sent her back to him."

"That's why it hurts you so much," she says, planting a kiss on my arm. "You feel guilty."

"Of course I feel guilty. This is how guilty people should feel. Guilty."

"He stole her from you first."

"That really doesn't make it better. I never even spoke to him after that day. Couldn't. I don't know if he even wanted me to call him. We were basically strangers by the end."

"You were family."

"When I got the call about the accident, I swore to myself, if he woke up from the coma, we'd talk it out. I'd tell him what happened, see if he still wanted to be my brother. But he never did wake up. Finally the doctors advised me to pull the plug."

"Oh my God."

"Right there in Regional Hospital, walking the same blue and red tiled floors that I walked to find you that night. They gave me a few minutes to talk to him before they did it. I could have told him then. It wouldn't really have mattered. They swore there was no brain activity. But then I thought, what if they're wrong. What if there's a chance they're wrong, and he hears me, but he can't swear at me. He looked so fucking small in that bed. He couldn't have punched me, and I deserved to be punched. So I didn't tell him. I walked away with that secret."

"Hey," she says, propping her chin on her palm. Her hair does this sexy flop thing onto my chest. "You had a toxic relationship with your brother. These things happen, but you are not a bad person. You were reacting out of hurt. You didn't mean to hurt him, and that you wish you could take it back... wherever he is, he knows that now."

Rhys is a bastard, and whatever hell he's in, I hope it burns. I don't tell her that. I don't tell her what I learned from Emily's diary the day after I pulled the plug on my brother. Instead I tell her, "You're going to make an incredible social worker one day."

A lopsided grin. "Really?"

I spell the letters on her shoulder. *Really.*

She's warm and sexy and everything I want in my very own bed, but I have things to do. People to see. Security to arrange. I can't pull her against me and ward away the cold.

"You need to sleep," I tell her. "Your eyes are already closing."

My sleepy girl rolls to her side, palm under her face as she watches me dress.

I find my jeans first. Then the shirt, which landed over a chair by the window.

She's already drowsing by the time I slip out of the bedroom. In the room next door, I check on Paige, but she's still sleeping. That's good. The doctors said that's normal. I should be sleeping too, and wouldn't I love being wrapped around Jane?

I can't let myself drift off in her bed. Look what happened last time. A fire. Devastation. *Death.*

Mateo is in the kitchen, which is predictable. He can usually be found wherever there's food, even in the middle of the night. It's something of a miracle that he stays as fit as he does, even with regular workouts. There's a plate of scones in front of him, a dish of clotted cream, but he's ignoring them in favor of his phone. There's some argument about what constitutes exclusivity in his contract with a major production company.

He sees me and ends the call. "My agent," he says.

"Want my lawyer to take a look at it?"

"Nah. They're just busting my balls because they want me to accept a bullshit offer for the sequel, but I'm going to hold out until they give me what I'm worth."

I grab one of the scones and scarf it down in two bites. "Would you have ever imagined the two of us like this back when we were sharing a shithole?"

"This was the plan. Getting rich. Taking over the goddamn world."

Wind knocks some flowers outside against the window. "Remember a few years back you had that nutjob stalker? The one who sent you dead animals?"

"I try to forget about that honestly. I still shudder when I see a raccoon."

"The cops ever find the guy?"

"There was a profiler who thought it was a woman. And no. After a while, the packages stopped coming, and there was no reason to continue. They said maybe she found a new target."

"The fire chief thinks the fire may have been set on purpose."

No change in his expression. That's why he gets paid the big bucks for acting. "Damn."

"Yeah."

"Who the hell did it?"

"I don't know. Maybe no one. Could have

just been an old house."

"But you don't think it was."

There's a bar in the restaurant. I wander there to pour myself a shot of whiskey, ignoring the throb of my leg. It's worse after fucking Jane, but I wouldn't take it back for anything.

Mateo follows me, waiting patiently for me to explain. It's not amazing whiskey. It burns all the way down. "I don't know, but I don't want to take any chances with Paige or with Jane. Whoever did this, whatever their motives, they clearly don't care about hurting the people near me."

"Why do you assume you're the target?"

"There were three people in that house. I'm definitely the biggest asshole."

"I won't argue with that." He glances toward the stairs. "Jane?"

He means, *maybe Jane set the fire.* Part of me revolts at the mere suggestion. I want to snarl in her defense, but I force myself to remain calm. "She came in after me. She didn't have to. Those aren't the actions of someone who wants me dead. I could have breathed my last if she hadn't been there."

"You're wrapped up in her pretty hard."

"Am I?"

"She's going to get hurt."

"Don't make me punch you in the face." He means that I'm going to hurt her emotionally, although I'm well aware that she also might be physically hurt. She could have died in that fire just as easily as I could have. "She's the nanny, and sure I have a soft spot for her. I also have a soft spot for the kitten Paige loves. It doesn't mean anything."

His look calls me a liar. "Then who do you think set the fire?"

"You're going to think I'm insane."

"I already think that."

"Remember when we would party in LA? If I died back then, who got the money?"

"Your brother."

"You know that, but what would everyone else think? We hadn't spoken to each other in years. Everyone knew he stole my woman. Anyone would think I'd rather give the money to a random charity than him. Or maybe some stripper who showed me a good night."

"So you die, your money disappears." Awareness sharpens his gaze. "But now everyone would know that it goes to Paige. She's an heiress basically."

"And whoever has custody of her controls the

money."

"So who gets custody of her if you die?"

"That's the thing. Joe Causey fought me for custody. He's her uncle, technically. The estate was modest enough when her parents died, but now that it includes my money, it's a goddamn fortune."

"Fuck. Can you make it so someone else gets guardianship if you die?"

"Not really. I can name someone in my will, but it's the courts who decide who gets her—and they're going to choose family first. Especially since he's local. And it gets worse. He's the detective assigned to the case."

"Are you telling me the person investigating the fire may be the person who set it?"

"I'm telling you it's a possibility."

He takes the bottle of whiskey and pours himself a drink. "This is insane."

I gulp down the rest of what's in my glass. "Yes."

"Did you tell the higher ups about this?"

"Yes, but it's a small department. There aren't a surplus of people available to investigate. And the police chief is good friends with Joe Causey. They go fishing together."

"This is fucked up."

"All I'm saying is, if you have a minute before your next movie starts, I'd like it if you could stick around. Doesn't hurt to have another person I trust around."

"Sure, man. But you know, it could have been me. I could have wanted to get back at you after our argument." His eyebrow rises. Maybe he thinks I'll take a swing at him. Maybe he thinks I'm stupid.

"If you were trying to kill me, you missed your chance. Back when we were partying in LA, when I'd get so fucking wasted I didn't know where I was, you were the beneficiary of my will."

"Christ," he says, holding his chest as if wounded. "I was an heiress and didn't even know it."

"Turns out you did have something in common with Isabella Bradley," I say, naming the gorgeous young woman he once dated. She was heir to a massive hotel fortune. Tabloids had a field day snapping photos of them. No one knew that theirs was a fake relationship. A carefully orchestrated farce between a party girl who wanted guys to stop hitting on her and an actor who needed a break from the speculation to focus on his work.

Mateo gives me the middle finger.

I pick up a thick linen card with my name scrawled across in feminine handwriting. *Beau Rochester.* "What's this?" I ask. "The bill?"

"That reminds me. Marjorie took a call for you. Seemed pretty upset about it. I was tempted to open it and read what it said, but I figure you'll just tell me."

Inside there are words written in quotation marks, as if they were being transcribed exactly as they were spoken. "*You're going to ruin her life, the same way you ruined mine.*"

My heart thuds in my chest. Blood rushes in my ears. "What the fuck is this?"

Mateo takes the note from me, but I don't need to see it to know what's there. There is a name scrawled beneath the words. Zoey Aldridge. She's the one who left the message. Apparently she hates me. I probably deserve that.

"Christ," Mateo mutters, tossing the card aside. "She's crazy."

"I dodged a bullet."

Mateo looks thoughtful. "Or what if you didn't. I thought she went back to LA. What if she didn't? What if she's the one who set the fire?"

Alarm runs through my veins. "She uses a private jet. We'll find out where it is."

"Either way, this is a crazy fucking message."

"She's right though."

"Don't go there, man. Don't let her fuck with your head."

"You said it yourself. I'm not the obvious kind of bad, remember? I'm the kind you don't see in the fog until it's too late. Except it's not too late for Jane."

CHAPTER ELEVEN

Jane Mendoza

AFTER AN HOUR of looking through boxes, I've found the little silver top hat and the wheelbarrow. The only red hotels and green houses I found have been melted out of shape. They're charred black. Somehow the cards for Pennsylvania Railroad, Baltic Avenue, and Marvin Gardens managed to escape relatively unscathed. There's also a handful of crumpled, fire-tinged hundred-dollar bills.

I collect this into a sad-looking pile the way a raven would make a nest.

We'll never find enough pieces to make it playable, of course, but I think about framing what's there. It will be an heirloom for Paige to keep.

Possibly the last physical remnant of her father.

Like the photo I had of my father.

The boxes are stacked in the back patio of the inn, a place with a floor and a roof but no outside walls. A stiff wind would blow everything important away, but we don't want to bring them inside. Not with the incredibly strong scent of smoke emanating from them.

While I'm working here, Paige plays in the garden. I called the little toy shop where we bought the paints and they delivered a new set. She's been painting the gnomes that are used liberally throughout. They were a very boring gray stone before. I hope they don't mind too much that they're now bright and cheerful with oranges, reds, greens, blues, and pops of pink. It's really my job to stop her from defacing private property, but she's had such a rough time lately, and she's finally showing curiosity and interest, that I figure it's worth the replacement fee.

I'm pretty sure children aren't allowed at the Lighthouse Inn, usually.

Pets aren't allowed either, but that doesn't stop Kitten from trying to pounce on lizards. So far she's caught zero of them. She's definitely made to live in a cushy household like Beau Rochester's, because she would not survive a day in the wild.

There are piles of boxes, but something dark blue catches my eye.

The diary. I pick it up. Somehow it escapes the fire unscathed, its pages damp from the firefighters who put out the fire. The velvet cover hasn't even been singed.

I flip open the pages, touching the script.

We went on a picnic today, R, P, and me. It was nice, almost like we are a real family. Outside the house it almost seems like we love each other.

Nestled in the pages are photographs taken with a polaroid camera, the saturated-color square set in a white border, elegant black scrawl in the space beneath. There's a beautiful blonde woman with ice-blue eyes. She stares at the camera, glamorous and unsmiling. The man beside her wears a suit. He has Beau's features, sharpened and refined. If Beau is the wild, craggy cliffside at the Coach House, this man is the manicured coast near the inn.

First anniversary, the beautiful handwriting says. There's no happiness between the two people in this photograph. The next photo shows the same couple in different clothes, just as beautiful, just as pristine, holding a young child.

Paige. Her face was cherubic, her eyes blank. She wore a dress so frilly and full of lace that it makes me itch just to see. *First birthday,* the scrawl says.

I flip through the journal with increasing urgency, feeling her dread rise, her insecurity over her marriage, her distance from her child increase.

> *R hit me today. Actually hit me. I was too shocked to say anything.*

Oh God.

"Jane."

I stand up in a rush, dumping the diary back into the box, shoving something nondescript and half-burned on top of it. Guilt rises in my throat. I should not be reading that.

Marjorie walks out, her red hair blowing in the wind.

"How are you?" she asks, her smile bright. I'm guessing she hasn't seen the gnomes.

"Hello," I say, gesturing to the boxes as a distraction. Pretty sure this is how magicians make you miss the fact that they're not cutting a person in half. Misdirection. "We're doing okay. I'm looking through them now. We should be able to get them out of the way soon enough."

She gives a small laugh. "Oh, that's okay. You know Beau Rochester is paying good money for the use of the property, including the patio."

"Right. Money." She has what I've learned is the Maine accent. She says Rochester like *Rochestah* and property like *prah-perty*.

A broken teacup sits near the top of an open box. Marjorie leans down to pick it up. "She used this set for afternoon tea. She loved formal gatherings like that."

"You mean Emily Rochester?" Her image flashes in my mind, the exquisite features, the perfectly curled blonde hair, the eyes that hold infinite sadness.

She gets this faraway expression. "We were friends."

"I didn't realize. I'm sorry."

"We weren't exactly close, but it was still a blow when she died. She was so full of life." Her pale blue gaze finds Paige in the garden. "And Paige still so young."

There's a wrench in my heart. "I'm very sorry."

She looks at me. "I'm glad they found you. It's almost like a little family. If I saw you with them, I would assume you were her mother. Young, of course, but still."

Heat floods my cheeks. I don't want to feel pleasure at her words.

I don't want to hope for more, considering I'm the hired help. Not part of their family at all.

I thought I could have this—what? This secret relationship, this sex with Beau Rochester and not fall for him. I was wrong. I mumble something about how I'm happy to help Paige through this difficult time. And I add, "I'm sorry about the gnomes."

A small laugh. "Rochester paid more than enough to cover them. It's incredible really. A kid from around here—" *Around he-ah.* "Becoming that kind of rich."

"It's wild." Not that I would know. Sure, I live in the inn. I eat food he bought. I wear clothes paid for with his money. It's all temporary. None of this is mine.

"Not like us," she says.

My stomach clenches. I'm like her—the people Rochester pays to do what he wants. He may be generous with his money, but it's still his. It's still our job to keep him happy.

To let his niece paint the garden gnomes.

Or in my case, to let him have sex with the nanny.

Bile rises in my throat. What if he considered the sex part of my job? What if he considered it his due for paying such a nice salary at the end?

"Yeah," I say, choking on the word. "Not like us."

Marjorie says something about good Maine hospitality. I'm supposed to let her know if I need anything, but most of all, if Paige needs anything.

When she leaves, I pull out the diary again. She's becoming a three-dimensional person to me, Emily Rochester. She's not only Paige's mother. Not only the woman Beau used to love. Now she's someone with her own hopes and dreams, her own fears.

It's her private diary. Her thoughts. Her secrets. Not meant to be shared with anyone, but definitely not with me—a complete stranger. I shouldn't even show this to Beau, honestly. It would probably only enrage him to find out that Rhys had hit Emily.

I'm reading the pages faster and faster, skipping more of them every time. Going through her pregnancy and her troubled marriage and her final days...

R guessed the truth today. He figured out that my weekend trip happened when I got pregnant. Paige looks just like him. They have the same eyes. I don't know what made him suspicious, but he lost his temper. I'm afraid for myself. I'm almost afraid for

Paige. Maybe she's not safe from him if he knows she's actually B's child. He looks at us with pure venom in his eyes, like we're the enemy. It's always quiet in the house now. It feels like a storm is brewing.

My heart pounds when I put the book down. That's the last line she ever wrote in this diary. *It feels like a storm is brewing.* Whether she meant a figurative storm or a literal one, she decided to go out on a boat with Rhys. Her husband. Did he hurt her? Did they have an argument that ended in the worst possible way? Was she fighting for her life on that harbor?

There's a knot in my stomach. She's not Beau's niece. She's his daughter.

Does he know? He must know. Nine months after they slept together, a child was born. He had to have wondered. Why did he let her grow up in another man's house?

Why was he so reluctant to claim her?

I don't know why it's hitting me so hard, the fact that Beau might be Paige's true father. Maybe because I lost my father. Maybe because I'm not over it, I'll never get over it. I don't have a family. Not my father, and definitely not Beau. I'm alone, and the realization hits me like a very poorly timed tidal wave.

I was fooling myself to think we could play house.

The red bricks that form the back patio turn into wavy lines. I feel like I might throw up. This is bad. I don't know if I can pretend, if I can rewind the last fifteen minutes in my mind.

I should have been more afraid of that blue velvet diary. Not because it holds Emily Rochester's secrets. Because it holds everyone else's secrets, too.

Paige runs over to me, covered in paint. I feel like I'm a robot going through the motions as I bring her inside and wash her face in the kitchen.

"Are you okay?" Marjorie asks. "You look kind of green."

I'm really not okay. My breathing comes fast. I really think I might vomit. How can reading a few words change everything so much? I feel like I don't know Beau Rochester at all. Of course I don't know him. We had sex. It doesn't mean anything.

God, why did I think it meant anything?

Then Mateo is there. He puts a hand between my shoulder blades, making gentle circles. "Hey," he says. "You've been working too hard, probably. Smoke inhalation is nothing to play around with. Do you want to go upstairs and rest? I'll watch

Paige."

I offer a weak laugh. "I think… I think I might have eaten some bad seafood. Maybe some fresh air will clear things up. Do you think you can watch her for a few minutes?"

"Of course. Should I get Beau?"

"No," I say, and then more gently. "No, I really just need fresh air."

I stumble out of the inn and down a gravel path. It leads to the beach. Not the rocky cliff that the Coach House had. There are sand dunes and reeds and a foamy line of water.

Wind whips my hair around my face, making me blind.

The water would be freezing right now, and that sounds like bliss. It would be freezing, so cold that I could be numb again. I'm already retreating inside myself, becoming who I was before I set foot in Maine. I let myself feel far too much with Beau—curiosity and desire and comfort. I let myself fall for him, and now I'm going to crash against the rocky cliffside.

"Jane."

I turn, and there's Beau, as if I conjured him with my thoughts. "Mr. Rochester."

His voice comes gently over the wind. "So now I'm Mr. Rochester again."

"You've always been Mr. Rochester."

"What's wrong?"

"Nothing." I thought I could live with his coldness, with his secrets, with his guilt. As if I'm some kind of mature woman, able to handle men who are black holes. I'm not Zoey Aldridge who can walk away with her chin held high. I'm going to get sucked into him. I'll never be part of that three percent of kids who age out of the foster care system who graduate college. I'm going to die on these cliffs. The certainty sinks into me, with equal parts fear and resignation.

"Jane."

A small, hysterical laugh escapes me. "I don't know what I'm doing here."

"Freezing to death, possibly. Let's go back inside and sit by the fire."

"Did you know she was your child? Paige?"

Silence. "I knew."

"Why didn't you do something before her parents—no, before Rhys died? She deserved to know who her true father was. She deserved to have both her parents."

"How the hell did you find this out?"

"Emily kept a diary." My voice is hollow. "I shouldn't have read it."

"By the time I found out, she'd already had

the baby. Paige was eight months old by then. She knew Rhys as her father. Emily seemed happy enough having a new baby. They were a family. Anything I would have done would have fucked it up."

"He was hitting her."

A muscle in his jaw moves.

"Emily. Rhys hit her when he got angry."

"I found that out too late."

"The diary?"

"I read it." A brittle laugh. "For all the good it did her, I read it when I arrived at the house. It was in her nightstand. It tells quite a story."

"You didn't know."

"Rhys was a bastard with me, because we were competitive and we were brothers and we hated each other just a little bit, but he would never hit a woman. He worshipped Emily. That's why I let him keep her. At least that's what I thought."

"I don't know what he felt for Emily, but I do know that men—even otherwise good men, men who love their families in every other way—can hit them." The secrets in the Rochester family feel like the fog, growing thicker and thicker. It's harder to breathe.

"I don't even know if he hit Paige. The diary didn't say."

My throat feels swollen shut. "I'm sorry."

"Don't apologize to me. It's my fault she's dead. I should have taken Emily out of that house. I should have claimed Paige as my own. I should have—"

"No." There are butterflies with wings made out of razor blades in my stomach. I clutch my hands around my middle as if to hold myself together. "Don't blame yourself for that. You didn't know what was happening in that house."

"She came to me, that weekend that Paige might have been conceived. She asked me to run away with her. I sensed a desperation in her, but I thought she had finally realized her mistake choosing Rhys. I thought she wanted me. I thought she wanted my money. I thought I could prove a point by fucking her and then sending her away the next morning."

I flinch. "You didn't know."

"That's the problem, Jane. I should have known."

I'm shaking my head. "Your brother is the one responsible for his actions."

"The only reason he pursued Emily was because I wanted her. Because of our rivalry. Any way you look at it, I'm the reason she's dead right now."

"Beau."

"I'm not Beau whenever you want, sweetheart."

"Mr. Rochester. It wasn't your fault."

"One woman is dead because of me. You might be next." He moves as if to touch me, and I flinch back. I can't let him touch me again. It will feel too good. It will always feel too good, except when I face reality. That's when it hurts. "I'm a monster who destroys everything I touch. And you and I both know I touched you. Thoroughly."

"Stop trying to scare me."

"Is it working?"

"No, God help me. I trust you anyway."

"Jesus Christ. When you are going to see? I'm the boss. You're the nanny. We're fucking because it's easy. It's convenient. Like eating leftovers because they're in the fridge."

I flinch. "No. You don't mean that."

His face goes dark and cold, almost the way he looked when I first met him. "You thought we were going to be a couple? That we were going to get married?"

"No, but I thought we cared about each other."

"You don't give a fuck how I feel about you

when I have my thumb against your clit."

A slightly manic laugh escapes me. "That's true enough. I would have thought I was a strong person. A principled person. And I am, except when you touch me. Then I become someone I don't even recognize."

"Is it so fucking wrong, then? Having sex?"

"It is when I'm locked in for a year. I can't leave, but you can fire me anytime. You told me that, remember? You can fire me anytime you want if I don't do a good enough job."

"You think I'll fire you if you don't suck my cock?"

I look down. "Why can't it be more? Why can't it be a relationship?"

His eyes have always been unnaturally opaque. Now they look as hard as granite. "Is that what you want? A public declaration? Maybe a little article in the tabloids?"

"I don't give a shit about the tabloids."

"What about the money?"

"I don't want your money."

"Everyone wants my money. That's the one true constant." When I make a sound of dissent, he snorts. "Even you. Do you want me to pay you the full amount right now?"

I press my lips together. Of course I do. Except there's no right answer here.

Everything is wrong, wrong, wrong.

"You aren't taking care of Paige out of the goodness of your heart. This is a transaction. It has always been a transaction. So don't bullshit a bullshitter. I see right through you."

Tears prick my eyes. Maybe he can see right through me. I feel like I'm made of tissue paper that's gotten wet with sea spray. I'm going to tear in half. He will see everything I'm afraid of— being left alone, having no family, going hungry. All of my fears exposed for him to ridicule. "Beau, I do care about you."

"Which one is it, sweetheart? Am I Beau or Mr. Rochester? Are you going to get down on your knees or are you going to spread your legs? Either way I'm getting what I want."

Pain lances through me. "Stop."

"No, you were right. I should be asking these questions. What are we doing together? As a nanny you're doing a great job, but as a fuck partner, well, let's just say I'm used to a little more excitement. So which one are you getting paid to do?"

Water and salt. I don't know whether it's the ocean or my tears. I lick my trembling lips. "We can't have sex again. I can't feel this way again."

A cold smile. "That answers my question."

"Beau—"

"What if I were to terminate our contract?"

"No."

"The irony is that it would be for your own good. Mateo warned me. He even warned you, not that it did anything. You thought you could make me fall in love with you."

"You said you loved me." *I love you, damn you.*

"I thought you were going to die. Now you're not. The moment passed."

I want so badly to be numb, to have that ice around my feelings. The words he's saying are like hot pokers, burning into my heart, leaving marks forever. "You're only saying this to protect me. To protect yourself." Tears make him a wavy form against the backdrop of the ocean. "Because you think you don't deserve to be happy. You do deserve it. I love you, Beau. *I love you.*"

"I've heard that before. Emily told me she loved me before I left for California. Then she fucked my brother." He gives me a hard look all the way down my body, a look that remembers every single kiss and touch we've shared together. "Rhys would have liked you."

It's a slap in the face. I stagger back as if it's

physical instead of just a handful of words. "This isn't you. And I'm not her."

"No," he agrees. "I would have taken care of her, even after she married my brother. If I'd known what was happening in that house, I would have taken her away. Protected her. Saved her. But you aren't her, are you?"

My tears feel like acid, burning my eyes. "Stop."

"I'm not going to terminate the contract," he says softly. "But then you already knew that. Because Paige needs you. And the craziest fucking part of all, I think I need you, too."

He turns and walks back to the inn, no limp whatsoever, leaving me reeling, the world tilting, my feet stumbling in the powder-soft sand, hardly able to breathe for how much it hurts.

He told me his love was dangerous.

Maybe he was telling the truth. It doesn't start fires. It doesn't start wars.

It breaks hearts. Mine feels shattered.

CHAPTER TWELVE

Beau Rochester

IT'S ONE THING to know the house burned to the ground. One thing to watch it coming down on top of us like hell turned inside out.

Looking at the charred remains is another thing entirely. I'm still not used to it.

I can see from the graveled drive where I stand at my car with my hands shoved into the pockets of my jeans. No person's looked at the ocean from this vantage point in a century. When it was first built, Coach House must have seemed like an intrusion. An unnatural barrier between the flat of the cliff and the view beyond.

Now its burned husk is a terrible compromise. It hasn't returned the land to its resting state, but it's not whole, either.

It begs to be rebuilt. Or leveled completely.

There's a hell of a lot more left than you'd

think would be in a burned-down house. Support beams slash through empty window frames like broken teeth. Ancient insulation boils over cracks in the walls. The roof collapsed down the center, leaving a clear path to the ocean.

The fire chewed up the house and spit it out.

It almost took me with it. It almost took Jane.

There's a sense that the house tried to eat itself to swallow its secrets. It would make me sound crazy to say it out loud. The house isn't sentient, but that's how it feels. It didn't do a particularly good job of the project, though. There's too much left. Too much scorched wood and blown-out insulation and paper scraps curled over everything.

Instead of consuming its secrets, it's exposed them—their charred remains floating in the salt-tinged wind, waiting for someone to read them.

It would be the most unsettling thing about today if I hadn't just left Jane on the beach.

Left her there, with tears in her eyes and her body half folded like I'd hit her. I didn't. I wouldn't. I'm not my brother. I'm not Rhys.

But that's bullshit, because I'm just as bad. Just as unpredictable. Worse.

I said that I didn't love her. I lied to Jane's face. What I said in the literal heat of the moment when the house was burning down was the truth, but I called it a lie.

What the hell kind of consummate bastard follows that up with *I need you?*

The kind I am, apparently.

I've been staring through the punched-out hole in the wreckage of the house for too long. It's not what I came here for. For several long moments, I can't remember why I came. Who gives a damn? I never should have walked away from Jane the way I did.

My first priority should be driving back down from the cliffs and offering her an explanation. But there's no explanation I'm willing to give. I won't subject either of us to that scene.

Paige is the one who needs her, not me.

And the last thing Jane needs is for her asshole of a boss to come knock on her door with his heart in his hands, begging for her kindness and her body.

She'd forgive me, too. That's the part that makes me feel sickest of all. That diary punched a hole through her understanding of the past. Then I said things that made it worse.

The things that came out of my mouth. Jesus.

I walk around the corner of the house, revealing myself to the wide-open landscape. The hair on the back of my neck stands up... as if someone's watching.

I glance along the line of the cliffs.

Along the tree line. Everywhere a person could be.

There's too much destruction to see anything clearly. In the bedrooms the inner walls stay partially standing. All it takes to get inside is pushing back damaged siding. It crumbles under my hands. A pocket watch peers out at me from the floor of the room. This was Rhys and Emily's bedroom. I push inside, and the feeling of being watched dissipates.

Paranoia brought on by stress. That's all it is.

My feet sink into the heat-weakened hardwood. If I'm not careful, I'll fall straight down to the cellar. Every footstep has to be considered. It doesn't take my mind off the prickling sensation all down my spine. If someone is here, on the property...

A gust of wind moves through the gaps in the structure. Its touch chills the back of my neck. Under my shirt. Everywhere under my coat. I feel like a ghost just walked through me. I feel like a ghost would have done less harm to Jane, unless it was a ghost who set the fire.

I've been back to the scene once before. A

deputy escorted me around while I threw whatever I could find into boxes to bring to the inn, but this is the first time I've had free rein.

Then I was restricted to the least damaged part of the house. Now I wade deeper into the area blackened and weak with fire, everything still smelling of smoke seven days later.

The glint of cherry wood reflects the sunlight through its layer of soot. I climb over rubble and unrecognizable burned furniture. It's my desk. Rhys's desk, technically. I didn't want to change too much when I moved in. Paige had been through enough changes in her life without also watching me redecorate her childhood home. But I'd never been completely comfortable in another man's home. Especially that man. My brother. We'd been competitive at best. Toxic and violent at worst. I always felt the lingering dark energy, a kind of subtle menace. The knowledge that he would fuck someone over if he could get away with it.

Somehow, the light has chased away that feeling.

Soot dances in the sun, surprisingly active, almost playful. Rooms that were heavy with history are now a pile of wood and fabric, made ordinary by ruin.

The fire was devastating, but one good thing came of it.

It cleansed the house, more effectively than a tidal wave.

The desk fell through the ceiling of the dining room. I climb over singed chairs and the large, cracked table to get there. My leg protests every goddamn crater. I used to ski the black diamonds in Vail. Now I'm reduced to leaning heavily on disjointed furniture to move around. When I first fractured my leg, it was a straightforward recovery. The strain of the fire, of being trapped under a beam, has irrevocably fucked it up. I need weeks of bed rest, according to the doctors. Months of physical therapy. Instead I'd checked myself out against their advice the next day. Paige needs me. Jane needs me, too.

There were two large flat-screen monitors on the desk. My computer's tower underneath. None of that is anywhere to be seen. It's probably under some of this other debris. The papers I'd been working on are gone. Burned to dust, probably.

The bottom of the desk has crumpled like an accordion.

The top is still intact. I open the first drawer, revealing a keyboard that seems barely bruised from the fall. The next drawer used to contain manila folders stacked neatly. Now they're crammed full of papers spilling over each other. I pick up one piece of paper. It's the court documents granting me guardianship of Paige. Her birth certificate. I gather the papers roughly and stuff them into the manila folder. The fact that they managed to escape both the fire and whatever chemicals the firefighters used to douse the flames is a minor miracle.

"Not safe for you to be climbing around in there."

I make a sharp turn at the voice. My foot cracks through the floor and I almost drop the folder. It's not a ghost who stands outside the dining room window—or the wall where the window once stood. It's the fire chief. Hanging close behind him is the bastard Joe Causey.

"No, Chief," I say. "It isn't." Alan Diebold has been the fire chief in Eben Cape for about as long as I can remember. He's personally attended most of the fires in the area. People still talk about the one he missed. The old bookstore, down on the main street in town. He was in the hospital with a heart attack. "Just wanted to see what was left."

"Not much," Diebold says, his tone grim.

The corner of Joe's mouth turns down. He

steps back to let me climb out. He acknowledges me with a wordless grunt. I give him a short nod in return. That's about the extent of the politeness between us, and it's only for Diebold's benefit.

The fire chief is in his sixties. He must be on the verge of retirement by now, but his dark eyes take everything in the same as they did before. "Like I told you on the phone, the scene's been released. That means we've collected all the evidence we need to get. You're free to get a cleanup crew in here to see what you can salvage. I imagine you'll want to tear it down, start over. The property will be worth a pretty penny, even empty."

"Haven't decided yet," I say, my tone non-committal. I'm keenly aware that Causey is listening, aware that he'll use anything I say against me if he has the opportunity. I lead them a few steps away from the house, and they follow me. "What did the evidence say?"

"Arson," the chief says, his eyes solemn. "Traces of accelerant in the attic. Not near any of the origination points we'd expect for an accidental fire. No stoves or electrical points. You know we mostly see pranksters around here. Tourists starting bonfires that get out of hand. Not often we come across a case like this. Have a couple fire investigators under me, but I took this one myself. Known the two of you since you were babies."

My stomach clenches. Accelerant in the god-damn attic. I'd known it was possibly arson. Probably, if I were honest, but I was hoping it wasn't. "Appreciate it."

His eyes are an unearthly pale between bushy gray eyebrows. He settles a stare on me that sends a bolt of cold down my spine. "You didn't store anything flammable up there, did you?"

"Christ."

"I have to ask."

"The truth is I don't know everything that was up there," I admit, my voice gruff. "It was full of furniture and boxes when I got here. I never really looked through it all."

"Sad business," he says, staring at the ruins. "First she loses her parents. Then she near burns to a crisp. It's a good thing you stepped up. She needs you, Rochester."

Tension vibrates through the air. Does the chief know that he's taking sides in a conflict that goes back decades? Hell, he might. He's always seen too much with those pale blue eyes. He lifts a thick finger toward the sky. "That's where it started, in the back, near the outer wall."

There was a window in that part of the attic. There was nothing up there.

But *someone* was.

I didn't hear footsteps in the middle of the night. No soft creaks along old flooring. Never once during a storm, when the rain would have muffled the sound. If I wonder about it now, if I hear the haunting echo in my mind, that's just paranoia superimposing itself on my memory.

It's only because I haven't been up there in weeks. Months, maybe.

Can't remember the last time.

"When's the last time you'd say you talked to Em?" Joe says, his notepad out like it's normal as hell to ask about a dead woman. Even if that woman is his sister.

Of all the things I hate about Joe, this is the fact I hate the most.

He lurked in the background of my relationship with Emily. Bristling. Scowling. Watching me as if I posed some threat. He tried to catch me out for years, when it was Rhys who was the dangerous one. Of course he probably blames me for that, too. I blame myself for it. We all know she would never have ended up with Rhys if I hadn't left for the West Coast.

The wind from the ocean quiets. The whole

place is listening now, even the trees. Joe drags his gaze up off his notepad and arches an eyebrow in accusation.

"Emily's been gone for years," I say, and a muscle in the side of his jaw flexes. "Any conversation I had with her has nothing to do with this."

Alan clears his throat. "There are those in this profession who talk about the psychology of arsonists. Profiling, they call it. Don't know if I always buy into it, but if I did..."

I tense. "Yeah?"

"The location of the fire suggests the arsonist is more likely to be a woman."

My pulse drops into my fingertips. "How? A fire's a fire."

The fire chief cuts a glance at Joe. "Female arsonists more often set fires that are calls for help. Not for the attention, not for the love of fire. Not to become a hero pulling people out of the house. We find those kinds of fires in the kitchen, usually. On the ground floor."

A kitchen fire would have killed us all. The flames would have eaten through the ceilings to the second floor, running down electrical wiring and skittering up the walls before we could get downstairs. It would have meant jumping out second-story windows.

Or dying before we could.

No. This fire was meant to flush us out. To *chase* us out.

"Did you look into Zoey Aldridge?" I ask, biting out the words, forcing myself to say them. I don't want to believe she would set the fire. I didn't think she had that in her, but I'm not going to take any chances. Someone set that fire, and now it sounds like it was a woman. "And she left a threatening note at the inn."

"She has an alibi," Causey says. "Though I did have an interesting conversation with her. Seems you've left a string of broken hearts through LA. Plenty of women who'd like to bring you down. Plenty of women with motive."

"What about the insurance money?" I say, raising a brow. "You seemed pretty set on that when you tried to interview my nanny without a lawyer present."

"Guilty people don't need lawyers," Causey says, and I snort. They do when there are questionable cops like Causey around, people who love power more than peace.

Diebold clears his throat. "Money's always a motive. But I don't see how you could be hurting for half a million dollars when you got many times more than that sitting in your accounts."

I run a hand over my face. It feels grimy. Walking through the smoke-drenched house left a residue of soot on my skin. "So you're saying the fire was set in the attic. That means someone was inside the house. How did they get there?"

"Couldn't say," Diebold says. "We looked for signs of forced entry, but there wasn't much left. No lockpicking marks on the deadbolt, for what it's worth."

Christ. The thought of someone walking the dark hallways makes me go still. I was wrapped in bed with Jane. Paige was in her room, defenseless. Did the intruder open her door? Did they look at that sleeping child before they lit a match?

Joe taps his pen on his notebook. "When was the last time you saw Emily?"

"We've been over this," I say, my teeth gritted. "You want someone to blame for her death? Talk to Rhys. You were friends with him. He's the one who took her out on that boat. Everyone knows she never liked being on the water."

"That's right," Causey says, his tone cold. "Blame a dead man."

"This is ancient history. The only question we need answered right now is who set the fire. That's your job, Detective," I say, adding sarcasm to the title. "Paige is your niece. Maybe if you're concerned about her safety, you can focus on the investigation."

His eyes narrow, as blue as Emily's. As blue as Paige's. "You never gave a damn about her. Did you show up for her birthdays? No, you sent a goddamn card. A check."

Guilt swallows me where I stand. It merges with the bitter scent of ashes from the fire, with the sight of Jane's eyes filling with tears on the beach. There are a million things I'm sorry for, which is proof enough that I should leave Jane alone. "I came here to talk to the fire chief. You want to give me shit for being an asshole, you'll have to get in line."

Joe flips his notebook closed and claps Alan on the shoulder. "Keep me updated." He walks away over the ruts in the grass left by the emergency vehicles.

Alan shades his eyes and watches him go. "He's never been right since his sister died."

He was never right before that, either, but I don't bother correcting him. "Maybe it's a woman," I say. "Maybe not. But how do you know it's not some teenage kid crying for help?"

"I don't," Diebold says. "Could be anyone. That's not really my purview, but the police department usually shares their leads with me.

Not in this case."

"Because he has no leads," I say, my teeth clenched.

Diebold runs a hand over his arm. I have a vague memory that he was injured in a fire once, around the time he got his promotion. He had burns along his entire left side. They're covered up now in his uniform. "Spent some time going through the wreckage. When you live in a place like Eben Cape, something like this, it's personal. It was interesting that there weren't any signs of a break-in."

"You said yourself the fire destroyed every-thing. Including evidence."

He looks out at the ocean. "You say Emily Rochester never liked being on the water?"

"She hated it. Said it made her hair frizzy. And she got seasick."

"Always thought it was interesting they never found her body," he says, his pale watery gaze meeting mine.

"Lots of bodies don't get found after boating accidents."

"She would have known every way into the house."

Chills race over my back. "Are you suggesting she's still alive?"

"I'm not suggesting anything." He gives a sudden, slightly manic laugh. "Just the imaginings of an old man. I should probably do the department a favor and retire already."

In the stunned silence my mind processes the following facts: that Emily Rochester loved this house. She wouldn't voluntarily leave. She used to point at it when we walked the beach on the other side. I used to dream about buying it for her. Of course, it was Rhys that eventually did that. It was Rhys she eventually married.

Why would she let everyone believe she died?

My brother was an accountant. Not a fisherman or even a hobbyist boater. Emily didn't grow up around the ocean. And she got seasick.

Despite those things, they rented a boat.

They went out on the water and never came back.

"No," I say, the word drawn out and final. "I don't believe in people coming back from the dead. I don't believe in ghosts. We had a funeral for Emily Rochester. She's gone."

"I'm sure she is," Diebold says, sober now. "But whoever set that fire didn't go up in flames. They're walking around the cliff. Walking along the beach. Walking the same places as you and me, so take care of Paige. And take care of yourself."

I glance at the winding path where Joe Causey's black department-issued Taurus descends the winding road. "You don't think he's going to catch the person who did it."

He scratches his head. "I'm not entirely convinced it wasn't him."

CHAPTER THIRTEEN

Jane Mendoza

I GO THROUGH the motions of Paige's bath-time routine with an aching heart.

As if Beau reached in and twisted it as he left.

Every beat of my heart forces me to remember his words on the beach. The man who said those things was the casual, cruel boss I started working for, not the lover in my bed. After everything, it's still painful. I wanted to sink down to my knees in the sand and sob.

Not with Paige waiting in the house.

Not with everything feeling as tenuous as it did when I first got here.

Now she flips over in the clawfoot tub and kicks her feet. Paige was suspicious of the tub until the first time she tried it. Then she did a complete one eighty. "It's like a pool!" she'd said, eyes round with astonishment. "Or a hot tub. I'm a mermaid. Look at me, I'm a mermaid."

There's more than enough room for her to stretch out her legs. She sweeps one hand through the water and makes waves on the side of the tub.

"Ten more minutes," she says.

And I get it. There's a whole toy store in there for her. Everything we had sent from a little shop downtown to try and coax her in. Bubble bath that makes the surface of the water glisten with rainbows. Floating toys in the shape of boats. Bath paints, which seem like they'll defeat the purpose but remain miraculously out of her hair.

"Five minutes," I offer as a compromise.

My temples throb with the stress of the argument. Beau said he needed me. It didn't stop him from turning his back on me. He claimed he didn't mean it when he said he loved me. A moment that passed, he called it. I don't have the energy to fight him.

"Seven," Paige says, and dunks her head under again. She learned how to make deals while playing Monopoly. She'll make you an offer on St. Charles Place for more than it's even worth. It seems like a good idea until she captures her monopoly and bankrupts you a few turns later.

"Okay," I tell her when she resurfaces. "Seven minutes."

I step out into Paige's bedroom. Most times, she wants to be alone, so I give her space. I've already washed her hair. She'll be pruny soon, but I don't want to push her too hard. So I perch on the edge of the bed and listen to her drag the toy boats through the water. From the sounds of her dialogue there's a pirate ship in battle with a cove of mermaids. Kitten naps peacefully on Paige's pillow, undisturbed by the battle.

A movement outside the window catches my eye. I sweep back the curtain a few inches, expecting to see moonlight on waves.

There's someone out there.

A woman, walking slowly down the beach. I get the impression of blonde hair bleached white by the moon. A long, pale nightgown. Unease skips down my spine. The woman doesn't seem to leave footprints in the sand—or maybe I'm too far away to see them. It's almost like she's floating over the beach, drifting toward the water.

"How many minutes? How many minutes left?" A child's voice calling from the bathroom.

I look over my shoulder at Paige, who's skimming the boat toy over the edge of the tub. "Five minutes," I say, my voice sounding hollow. Afraid.

When I look back, the beach is empty. That

doesn't make me feel better. Not at all. She wasn't walking fast enough to disappear. I stick my head close to the window and look up and down the shore. No one's there.

I drop the curtain and rub my hand over my eyes. It was a traumatic event, the house fire. It's making my imagination run wild.

A trick of the light. That's all. Stress, and a trick of the light.

I go back into the bathroom. "Time to hop out and get dried off."

"Ten more minutes." Paige clings to the edge of the tub, only her eyes peeking over the side.

"I'm going to get your pajamas ready."

A new pajama set waits in the top drawer of Paige's dresser. I snap the tags off one by one and drop them into her little wastebasket.

"Ten more minutes," Paige calls, though I haven't been back to warn her. I shouldn't keep bargaining with her, but it's hard to be strict with a girl who's gone through so much. First losing her parents. Then a fire. Let her enjoy her baths, if that's what she likes.

"I'm almost done," I answer back.

A shadow darkens the door. His scent follows a moment later. Wind and ocean and... smoke. Beau watches me with dark eyes made darker by his thoughts. "Jane," he says.

My hands clench around the pajamas. "Paige is having her bath."

In the bathroom, she makes a noise like a cannon's blast.

Beau straightens up and clears his throat. Despite the strength of him, the ferocity of him, all contained in that muscular body, he looks... vulnerable.

Like he's recently been burned through as much as the house has.

"I need to apologize to you for my behavior earlier." Every word is stiff. Uncomfortable. "I shouldn't have said those things to you. I'm sorry."

Then he nods his head and turns to go.

I should let him. I should let him walk out of here and go change his clothes and stay my cold, distant boss. We could have the kind of neutral boss–employee relationship we should have had all along. His love is dangerous. He proved that to me on the beach.

But there's something about the set of his shoulders that speaks of loss. He's bereft. I don't know of what. The house? His old life? Or some other, more elusive spark?

I don't know, and I desperately want to know.

I move after him in a few quick steps. "Wait."

He doesn't say a word as I catch his arm in the hallway. Beau's dark eyes widen for a fraction of a second, and then his gaze slips down to my hand on his sleeve. The salt scent of the ocean is stronger here. His eyes have more depth. The light from the bathroom catches and recedes in their black centers. It's harder to breathe with him looking at me like that.

Like I'm some monumental decision for him to make.

My mouth has gone dry. "What did the fire chief say?"

His brows knit together into something like pain. He wants to lie. I can see it in his eyes. I can see myself reflected there, too. I'm dressed in all the expensive clothes he gave me. A piece of his world, now. On the surface, I fit in here, but I don't want him to hold me at arm's length. I don't want him to keep me out.

"Tell me the truth," I demand in a whisper. Halfway through it becomes a plea. "Trust me."

He brushes my hand away and backs me against the wall in a single pained heartbeat. Beau's big hand cups my jaw. It's not like it was on the beach. He's not pulling away from me. He's pushing in, hard, his mouth confident on mine. Hot on mine. Possessive. It's like he takes my words as a challenge, like the truth he offers is in every stroke of his tongue against mine, every ragged breath we share.

His other hand steadies my hip. My heart pounds at the contact. He can't hide from me like this. He isn't hiding from me like this. From the rest of the world, maybe. No one can see us here in the dim light of the hall. There's only the aching truth between us. He needs me. I want him.

Beau shoves a knee between my legs. My head tips back in spite of myself. *Keep silent.* I have to stay silent, though he's giving me just enough contact to light my nerves up from end to end. It's dirtier than touching me with his fingers. More shameful.

Part of me loves that shame. I would rather be ashamed like this every minute for the rest of my life than watch him stalk away from me again.

The thought of making that trade—my shame and submission for him to stay, stay, stay—tears a gasp right out of my mouth.

"That's it," he says, close to my ear. I shouldn't let him do this. I should stand up tall and demand to finish the conversation on my own terms. Demand more than a stiff apology from him. I can't even make an attempt at pulling my body away from his. I want it too much.

I let all my weight come down on his leg. Let his hand coax my hips into rocking against him. The rest of me follows. I want my hands in his shirt, my lips on the side of his neck. I want more of him. More of him than I can possibly have in the hall. More of him than I have time to take right now. I press a kiss to the side of his neck. Drag the tip of my tongue through the ocean-salt taste of his skin. Swallow another gasp.

It's only when I'm near frantic with the need to come that he pulls back, eyes dark with warning. "The fire chief said it was set on purpose."

It's humiliating, how close I am to coming. He delivers this news right as I go over the edge so I have no choice but to hear it while I shudder out the kind of needy orgasm that makes my face burn. It doesn't sate me. Not when it's followed so closely by awareness of what he said.

My nerves against his leg send me up and up and up again. He's doing it on purpose. He's making me come because he has more to say.

The horrible anticipation of it gets overrun by pleasure.

"Someone was in the house that night." His

steady voice has an edge of certainty. An edge of anger as he rubs me to climax. "Someone lit a goddamn match."

Shock moves through me, chasing down the pleasure. Fear comes next. Cold in my veins. Of course it was possible. Possible that someone else came into the house and started the fire. I hoped it wasn't. The idea that someone walked above our heads while we were sleeping—while we were having sex, even—makes my skin crawl.

I hadn't suspected a thing, so consumed by Beau Rochester.

Whoever it was, they took advantage of us. The memory seems violated somehow. I was in Beau's arms while someone plotted to kill us in his house.

I don't know what to do. Throw myself fully into his arms or step away? I can't do either one. I'm still pinned on top of his legs. His hands on my hips hold me in place.

He lifts a hand to my cheek. "Jane—"

"I want to get out." Paige's voice rises to a shrill shriek, and the slap of bath water hitting the floor comes a second later. "Jane. Jane. *Jane.*"

I untangle myself from Beau and cross back through the bedroom to the bathroom. Paige stands in the tub, arms crossed over her chest. It's the pose of an angry little girl but her face isn't upset. It's relieved, almost. Like I was gone a second longer than she could handle. I grab a towel off the hanger by the sink and hold it out, both arms wide.

Paige steps out of the tub and lets me wrap her in soft cotton. Her little shoulders look even smaller through the drape of the towel. "Where did we put that brush?" I muse, mostly to myself. Mostly to calm my racing heart. The hormone warmth of two orgasms heats my veins.

"In the top drawer." Paige draws the towel tighter around her as I retrieve the brush.

I focus all my attention on combing her hair. All of it, except the part that's still hearing Beau's words from the hallway. *Someone was in the house that night.* It's scarier than the fire starting. Knowing that someone was there. Someone else could have tiptoed past my room. Someone could have pressed their ear to the door, listening to us together.

Someone could have used that fact against us.

It occurs to me now that Joe Causey knew Beau and I had sex. He knew from the very first time I met him in the hospital. How did he know?

"Jane?" asks the small girl in front of me.

"Yeah?" I say, too quickly, smiling back a beat too late at Paige's reflection in the mirror.

"Can I have a glass of milk before bed?"

I shake off the urge to tell her no. I don't want to go to the kitchen of the inn. In the face of Beau's news, what I want to do is lock ourselves behind the nearest bedroom door and not come out until the police have found the person.

In the meantime, what if they come looking for me?

They could.

Someone was in the house that night.

"Of course you can." I won't show her my sudden, irrational fear. Beau has security systems installed at the inn. Nobody is going to get in here without tripping an alarm. It's perfectly safe for me to walk to the kitchen and pour Paige a glass of milk.

I run the brush through her hair one more time, sweeping it back from her face.

Paige studies me in the mirror. "Jane?"

"Yeah?" There's no sense in upsetting Paige with this, so I give her my biggest, warmest smile.

She smiles back. It's not a full-on cheesy grin, but after all she's been through, I can't say I'd expect it. Paige's smile squeezes my heart. "Can we play Monopoly tomorrow?"

CHAPTER FOURTEEN

Beau Rochester

MARJORIE STARTLES WHEN I enter the kitchen. Her shoulders tighten at a board creaking under my foot, and she snaps her head around with wide eyes. "Mr. Rochester."

She's rinsing her hands in the sink. The dish towel she reaches for has been ironed and hung neatly over a hook near the sink. She's the kind of innkeeper who pays attention to details like dish towels matching the drapes.

I imagine it's one of the only things we haven't disrupted.

"Is there something I can do for you?"

My own blood pounds in my veins. I want to go back upstairs to Jane. I want to take her face in both my hands and kiss her the way I would if we had all the time in the world. "You took down a message for me. I need to know more about it."

Her hands flutter down to her skirt. Emotions cross her face in rapid succession—fear, defiance, guilt. The guilt is interesting. "I didn't want to write it down."

"But you did."

"It was crazy." She meets my eyes with a kind of desperation. Marjorie's not the type to get mixed up in anything like this. She runs a tight ship at her inn. It doesn't matter that I wouldn't blame her for someone leaving a message. "I decided to throw it away while I was out, but you already found it by the time I got back."

The same prickling paranoia I felt at the house taps the back of my neck. "What did she sound like? Were there any noises in the background?"

Marjorie's eyes get wider. "Do you think she would come here to find you? I just assumed she was one of your—" A flush creeps up her cheeks.

She's talking about the photos of me that made it to the tabloids.

Damn those photos.

At the time, being photographed like that felt like success. It felt like I'd finally arrived. It painted a picture I didn't mind. That I enjoyed a beautiful woman every night in my bed. That I had the money and skill to be sought-after. It was such hollow bullshit compared to what I want now—only one beautiful woman.

Jane. Upstairs right now. Cheeks stained pink from how I made her come in the hallway, backed against the hall. Off-limits. Completely off-limits.

The more times I run up against that limit, the more I want to tear it down. I've already blasted through it more than once. Always swearing it will be the last time.

It's never the last time. Even now, I'm dying for the taste of her. This kitchen seems like another world compared to the dark upstairs hallway. Compared to her bed.

"You didn't hear any sounds in the background that would tell you where she was? Anything at all? People in an office? At a club? The ocean? A train?"

"No. I thought you knew who she was. She left her name."

"Zoey Aldridge claims she didn't call."

Her pale green eyes widen. "I don't think—"

"Any other voices, even. Anyone trying to speak to her." I don't know what it would tell me even if someone had stood behind the mystery caller and whispered an address. She could be anywhere, calling from any cell phone, with anyone else on the planet.

But any information is better than no information. I can't live in this house knowing that I've left a stone unturned when it comes to figuring out who the hell is after us.

And proving that it's not Emily back from the grave to haunt us.

It sounds utterly ridiculous. And somehow reasonable at the same time.

Emily is dead. It's why I have custody of her daughter. There's no such thing as ghosts, but stranger things have happened in the world. They never found her body.

But if so, why the hell would she light a fire in the house where her daughter slept? Every time I turn this around, I find another angle that doesn't fit. The only thing that fits is the fear sinking to all the low points in my blood. It's here to stay until I can solve this.

"I'm not sure, Mr. Rochester. I can't say." Marjorie bites her bottom lip with her teeth. Her gaze glances furtively to the old-fashioned rotary phone. "I'm not sure I want to say."

The worry has sunk so deep in my bones that anger takes hold easily. It lances over my knuckles. First Joe Causey being an asshole over at the house, and now Marjorie, wanting to keep things from me.

Secrets are deadly. She should know that.

"You don't want to say what?"

"I don't know anything about the woman who called." She squares her shoulders. Lifts her chin. "The only person I know about in this situation is you."

"What do you know about me?" Nothing, except that I'm Rhys's brother. Nothing, except for what the rest of the town already knows. In a place like this, it's impossible to keep the past under wraps. I know what Marjorie's going to say before she says it.

"That you break hearts." How the hell has this conversation gotten to this place? "Not just that woman's, but Emily's too." The corners of her mouth turn down, and her gaze slips to the floor for a brief instant. "She loved you, and you left. If you had stayed, she never would have married your brother." Marjorie takes a deep breath as she reaches her inevitable point. "If you had stayed, she would still be alive."

"I'm not the one who killed her. Blame her husband who took her out on the boat. Blame the ocean." I keep my tone level, but she's right. If I had stayed, Emily would still be here. I would never have had to seek out a nanny agency. I would never have met Jane. "I came for details about a disturbing message you wrote down. Not accusations."

I've made those same accusations to myself enough times. I've bought into the stories in the tabloids enough times. I don't need to hear them now, when everything that matters to me in the world is in danger from an enemy who doesn't want to show her face.

Or his face. Joe Causey is the one who keeps showing up, time after time. To ask me about the house. To ask me about Jane.

Marjorie looks like she wants to say more. She doesn't. She presses her lips together, gives me a curt nod, and leaves the room. I'm across it in two long strides, opening up the cupboard above the sink. Scotch. A glass. The shift in the air happens as I pour the scotch. It makes my shoulder blades go tight.

"How much did you hear?" I ask the empty room.

The kitchen's empty, but not the hall outside. I knew it as soon as Marjorie left. Jane steps into the doorway, her arms clasped around her belly. "Enough."

I down the scotch. "Enough for what?"

"Enough to know why you keep pushing me away." I could listen to her voice, calm and low, for the rest of my life. Except when I want her to moan for me. Except when I want her to make those breathy little noises that make my cock twitch. Except for then.

"Because you're so many years younger than me?"

"Besides that."

I put my glass down on the countertop. I'll wash the damn thing out again as soon as I'm finished with this conversation. And I hope this conversation never ends. "Because you're employed by me, and I'm probably breaking a hundred laws just thinking about what I want to do to you right now?"

"Besides that."

"Do we need another reason?"

She comes to me, and in her dark eyes I see a sweet compassion that a man like me will never deserve. Not if I spent a hundred years making things up to her. "You're afraid I'm going to get hurt," Jane says softly. "I wouldn't leave in the fire, but it's more than that. You feel responsible for what happened to her."

I turn my back on her and the truth. Can't look at her for another second. It's too heavy a responsibility alongside everything else, and it hurts. It feels like she's pushed a knife through my ribs. I can feel the point digging into my heart.

Next I'll hear her footsteps, retreating out of the room. Jane will go back upstairs. We won't have to talk about this. We won't talk about the way I'm trying to shut her out again. The kitchen furniture—a single table and four matching wooden chairs—feel like an audience. I want fifty locked doors between me and Jane and the rest of the world.

Her body meets mine instead. Jane wraps both her arms around me from behind. It makes me shudder. It's clean, pure desire, shot directly into my veins. I wish I could lift a car or climb a mountain. Something, anything to do with this lust. Anything but fuck Jane on the pristine countertop of this inn. It would be nothing to lift her up and angle her the way I want to. It would be nothing to push her thighs apart and stroke across her center so I could feel how she's still wet from when I made her come. She would be. She is now. I know it.

Jane's hand moves over my chest, tempting and hesitant too, and the innocence of the gesture makes me harder. I can't push the feeling away. I can't push her away. It's like an ocean swell. You can fight it, but you'll tire yourself out and drown. Almost always better to let the current take you where it wants to go and wait until you're on shore to do battle. So I ignore the warning in the back of my mind and turn in her arms to face her.

"You're right." I brush my knuckles over her throat, the bones iron hard against velvety softness. Jane swallows as I do it. "I don't want you to get hurt. And there's someone out there who wants to kill us. Who already tried."

"Zoey Aldridge?" A little frown at the corners of her mouth. Jane hated when Zoey was in the house. She tried so hard not to show it. I almost wish she would have so I could have seen her blush and lift her chin, the way she's doing now.

"Maybe. I have people looking into her whereabouts, but her private jet flew back to Los Angeles the morning after the dinner party. She's been in Hollywood, supposedly. If it was her, maybe she paid someone else to do it."

Jane frowns, as if she can't quite believe what I'm saying. As if, after everything, she doesn't want to believe the worst in people. But she knows better than that. Her life has taught her otherwise. "Does she hate you that much? Enough to pay someone to do that?"

I don't want to tell her the worst of me, so I don't. Not now. The smile barely makes it to my lips. "She's not the first woman to hate me. And she probably won't be the last. You should take it as a warning, Jane. I'm not good for you. Not good for anyone."

CHAPTER FIFTEEN

Beau Rochester

I MIGHT NOT be good for Jane, but that doesn't stop the night from rolling into morning. I feel pulled to the Inn. To this routine that Jane and Paige are starting to put together. Jane, who lost everything, is making something out of nothing for Paige.

Well—not nothing. I catch Jane noticing her new clothes. I catch her enjoying them. She runs her fingertips along the hem of her shirt and brushes a palm over the smooth fabric at her stomach. Like she can't quite believe they're so soft.

All morning, she and Paige are busy. They're coloring on the back patio. Painting at the dining table. Reading books curled up on the couch together.

Then, at lunch, Paige puts down her peanut

butter and jelly sandwich. "I want to play Monopoly now. You said we could."

The shiny new box arrived from Amazon already. It's not the exact version that Paige had, but I suppose she's desperate enough to play to accept it. "Right now?" Jane asks.

This is the most animated I've seen Paige since the fire. She seems colorful again. Alive. "Now," Paige says, her gaze settling on me. "I want you to play, too. I want all of us to play."

My instinct is to back away and let Jane and Paige inhabit the little world they've created. The one where they're safe from me. But Paige looks so hopeful. I still remember her standing in the night, the tarp wrapped around her as a makeshift blanket.

"Where are we playing?" I say, resigned.

Paige grins at me. She scrambles down from her stool at the kitchen island and runs up the stairs two at a time. She comes back down a minute later with a series of thumps and goes to the wide coffee table in the middle of the living room.

Marjorie keeps the space neat and clean and comfortable. I'm glad to have the whole place to ourselves. Paige needs as little friction in her life as possible right now. Letting her choose where we play and where we sit without outside interference is good for everybody.

Jane puts the plates into the sink and follows her, and I follow Jane, my hands aching to touch her. Paige stands at the coffee table, the game in her hands, peering suspiciously at the set. "This isn't right," she says.

"Let's open it up and see." Jane takes the game from Paige, opens the plastic wrap with a fingernail, and puts the box on the edge of the table.

Paige slides the top off and purses her lips at the piece. "It still doesn't look right."

"It's not the same set as you had before," Jane agrees. "It will be different. But the rules will stay the same."

"What if they're not the same?" Paige frets as Jane sets out the board and unwraps the stacks of cards from their plastic. "What if they changed the rules and changed everything about it?"

"They didn't change everything about it," Jane says. She sits down on her footstool and picks up the first piece. "See? Here's the shoe and the top hat."

Paige tests them in the palm of her hand. "They don't feel right." Her cheeks get red, and Jane puts a hand on her elbow. "They don't feel right at all. I think they're different. They're too different. Look at this, there's a dinosaur. There shouldn't be a dinosaur in Monopoly."

"It's hard when things aren't the way we expected," Jane says. "You wanted the pieces to be the same, but this isn't your old game. This one's new, and it has different parts. But the rules are still the same. We'll still have a fun time playing together."

"I don't want it like this," Paige says, but her voice stays quiet. She's not preparing to scream. Instead she takes a breath in through her nose and lets it out through her mouth. "The pieces are different."

Jane smiles at her, pride shining on her face. "But the rules are still the same."

"Okay," Paige says. "Okay." She puts the shoe and the top hat on the board and looks over the cards, seeming to take comfort in the familiar colors and names of the properties.

I take a seat on the couch and Jane pulls up a footstool to the other side of the table. Paige stands at one end, and we set up the board. Paige is the banker, naturally. And the little silver top hat. She decides that I'll manage the real estate cards. That leaves Jane to control the little green houses and red hotels. I pick the battleship and

Jane picks the cat. She nudges the dinosaur out of sight. Paige has had enough change for the time being.

Paige rolls the dice on her first turn. "This is what families do," she says, her voice carefully nonchalant. "They play games together. We're like a family."

Jane's eyes meet mine from across the table, and then she's looking back at Paige. "It is kind of like a family. How do you feel about that?"

"I like it," Paige admits, and my heart clenches.

The truth is I like it, too. More than is safe for me to admit.

Paige rolls first. She lands on Chance. The orange card allows her to advance to the nearest railroad. That puts her on Pennsylvania Avenue. "I don't know," she muses. "Railroads are tough because there's no way to build houses even if you get a monopoly."

"You could pass," Jane says.

"I'd buy it," I say because I'm more comfortable spending this bright paper money. I'm also more comfortable spending real green money. Jane's much more nervous about spending. And Paige? She's strategic. She focuses on building monopolies.

Jane rolls next. She lands on Oriental Avenue, where she pauses to look at her money and consider the cost, but ultimately decides to buy it.

"Are we a family?" Paige asks.

Jane's hand freezes on its way to take the card with the pale blue strip for Oriental Avenue then keeps going. "Beau's your family," she says, keeping her tone light.

Kitten chooses this moment to run across the room and hop up onto the table in the middle of the board, knocking my battleship over. Jane picks the kitten up and deposits her back on the floor while I put my piece upright again.

On the outside, I probably look calm.

On the inside, I'm reeling.

Are we a family? I'm struck that Paige would ask the question. And I'm struck by how strong my desire is to say yes.

"What about you?" Paige looks between the two of us. "Are you like a mom and dad?"

Jane swallows. "We both take care of you. You can trust us and ask for help. That's something we have in common with moms and dads."

Her questions hit a deeper nerve.

Something I try to keep at the very back of my mind.

Paige might be my daughter. I might be her

father. I've always known it was possible, based on when Emily visited me. When we slept together. Regardless, I thought she was better growing up with a real family—with Rhys and Emily. Sitting here with her now, I could convince myself that she's mine. She looks a little like me. She has a temper like me.

She's good with money like me, even if it's Monopoly money.

I roll double fives, which puts me in the "Just Visiting" part of jail.

Paige watches my every move. If it were true, what would it even mean? Should I get a DNA test? Would it matter, since I'm already her guardian?

Even if I had the hard evidence, I could never tell Paige.

She always knew Rhys as her father. I won't take that away from her.

It would hurt her, and the thought of causing her any more pain makes my chest ache. Having to witness her grief at losing her mom and dad was the hardest thing I've had to see. To find out Rhys wasn't even her father would rival that. It would be like losing him twice.

"You're like my replacement dad," Paige says.

"I am." There's not really much point in

denying it. I'm the closest thing to a father she'll ever have now that Rhys is gone. Would it be so wrong to lean into that idea?

Becoming her guardian terrified me at first. Kept me up at night. How the hell was I supposed to know what to do? It kept me up at night, how badly I failed her in the beginning. I'm not sure I'm succeeding now, but there have been improvements.

Jane has been an improvement.

Paige plays with the dice in her hand. "There are supposed to be two parents."

"Not always," Jane points out. "Some people have single parents. Or live with only one parent. Every family is different, but the important thing is that there are people who love you."

"What if I wanted two parents? Would you stay?"

Jane's sweet brown gaze meets mine. She looks helpless, warmed by Paige's words, somehow hurt by them as well, because she thinks it isn't possible.

"Jane has her own dreams," I say, keeping my voice casual. "She's going to college. She's going to become a social worker to help kids who need it."

"She could be a social worker here," Paige

says.

She's stubborn. I'm sure she gets that from our side of the family. "Jane is only here temporarily. We talked about this when she got here, remember? How she'd stay with us for a year?"

Paige gives me a disappointed nod and the tension fades.

With a flourish, she rolls the dice. She lands on New York Avenue and buys it. We continue playing for a few rounds, buying up properties when we land on them.

Paige takes an early lead in the game. I'm not surprised.

She's damn good at the game.

What does surprise me is how much I want to be in this moment with her, and with Jane. It's easy to slip into this fantasy of thinking Paige is really my daughter.

It feels… warm to think about her like that. Right. And complicated.

Maybe my love doesn't have to be dangerous.

Having Paige with me has shone a light on all the pieces of me that are still bent or broken. The parts that still don't know what to do with all the complexity of the world. There's a certain guilt that comes with knowing I can't be perfect for her.

But there's also a deep sense of love. And in moments like this…

Happiness.

Paige is only seven, but that doesn't slow her down at Monopoly. She knows the rent on Pacific Avenue with three houses without even looking at the card. She calculates the amount to return when we give the bank money for property in the blink of an eye. The longer the game goes on, the more focused she becomes. She works to gather monopolies, and once she has them, she spends all her money to build houses. It's a smart strategy. She has less money than us right now, but all it takes is landing on her hotel once to bankrupt us.

Pretty soon she owns the entire left side of the board.

I could let her win. I wonder if that would make me a better uncle. Or a better father, a voice inside my head whispers.

Then again, she could probably tell if I threw the game. Why not give her a challenge?

She already owns the lower-cost side of the board, which I have to admit is the best position. It's easier to build houses and hotels. And everyone passing *Go* is likely to land on something before they pass Free Parking.

So I focus on the more upscale properties, the

yellows and greens. Soon I own an entire corner. I'm taking rent from the hand over fist with only a single house on each.

"You're a tough landlord," Jane says, mortgaging her properties to pay me.

"It's a cruel world," I agree, accepting the stack of fifties and twenties.

On the next turn, Jane lands on Baltic Avenue with a hotel. Paige's property. There's not enough unmortgaged property left to pay it, so she folds.

That leaves Paige and I battling it out.

There are moments it seems like she's going to win, but I'm lucky enough to land on Income Tax instead of her hotels. Paying $200 is cheaper than her exorbitant rents. She manages to avoid the now-called corner of doom by landing in jail, sending her back to safety.

In the final moments, my battleship is poised to enter her side. It seems almost impossible that I'll be able to get through safety another time. We're both evenly matched, but our properties are stacked so high that a single wrong move will end the game.

Then it's her turn. She's still on the orange spaces, in relative safely.

She rolls. It's a twelve.

Neither of us expected a pair of sixes. That

carries her all the way to Pacific Avenue, where she has to shell out $1,400 in rent. That puts a dent in her cash. She also has to sell off some houses, but she's still standing. I manage to avoid her spaces by landing on Community Chest.

Then she lands on the ultimate space—Boardwalk.

That wipes out most of her houses and requires her to mortgage some of her properties. With this much money in my coffers, the game is essentially over.

"You beat me," Paige says, sounding more surprised than frustrated. There's a kind of grudging awe in her eyes. "I usually win."

"I know you do. You get it from our side of the family."

"You did pretty good," Paige says. "Did you and daddy used to play?"

"We were pretty competitive," I say, which is an understatement. It was normal for our games to end in fistfights, the board pieces scattered as we threw punches.

"What about you?" she asks Jane. "Did you used to play when you were a kid?

I tense, wondering if the question will bother her. My childhood wasn't exactly sunshine and cookies, but it's nothing compared to hers. She lost her father and then got tossed around in a system rife with abuse. But she doesn't appear bothered by the question.

"Yes, and I lost then, too," she says, laughing. I would sit here playing Monopoly with her forever just to hear her laugh. "Wiped out. Flat broke. It's just like in real life."

CHAPTER SIXTEEN

Jane Mendoza

THE IPHONE IS the fanciest phone I've ever owned. It feels both sturdy and incredibly breakable in my hands, even protected in its shiny new case. I can't stop running my fingertips around the edges. It's beautiful, honestly. Too beautiful for a phone to be. And it's mine.

In my room at the inn, I have a few free minutes to spend with it. I didn't want to take it out of the box at first. It felt too much like the clothes. Too much like stepping into someone else's life.

Jane Mendoza can't afford the latest iPhone with its sleek, considered packaging.

Even opening the box felt nice. Peeling back the protective film on the screen was an upgraded experience. Ten minutes with it, and it already feels at home in my hand. It's easy to get used to this kind of thing. It's made to be that way.

I curl up on the bed and reset all my passwords while Paige plays in her room. She likes to have a few minutes before we start the day. And my hours don't officially start until eight.

It only takes a few minutes to log in to Facebook.

Notifications pop up the second the screen loads. Messages. For me. From Noah.

I haven't heard from you in forever—are you okay? Did something happen??

If you don't answer, I'm flying to Maine to make sure you're okay.

I'm dialing his number as soon as I read that last message. The last thing anyone needs is for Noah to fly to Maine in that state of mind. He'd find me in the inn, in clothes that we could never afford, and—

"Jane?"

"It's me, Noah. It's me."

He curses, relief and frustration tight in his voice. The background noise crashes next. Someone shouting in the background. He must be at his warehouse job right now.

"Don't hang up," he says over it, his voice broken by the pounding. A voice in the background swings close, then fades away. The rest of the noise fades with it until I can barely hear the thrum through the speakers. I know just how Noah would look, stepping out into a muggy Houston morning, hands shaking as he pulled out a cigarette to smoke. "What the hell happened?"

"There was an accident." Lie, lie, lie. It was no accident. Someone lit the house on fire while we were in it. It's been confirmed by the fire chief. "A fire. I lost my phone."

"What? What the fuck?" His breathing picks up. He'll be pacing right now. Walking away from wherever he's been. "Tell me what the hell happened, Jane. Tell me right now. Fuck."

"I'm fine." I'm not fine. Nothing is fine. The house burned down and I spend every day breathing in fear and frustration. "I'm okay. We all got out in time."

"The whole house?" He's horrified. "The whole thing came down?"

It came down on Beau first. Heat scorches my cheeks. His dark eyes had looked out at me from an ocean of orange. That beam pinning him to the floor. His fury, like a fire itself. *I love you, damn you*. He hadn't had enough leverage to save himself but he found it to shield me from the ceiling coming in. Every breath I take feels hot. Tight. My lungs ache.

"Yeah. The whole thing, and I lost—" Tears

sting the corners of my eyes. I've stayed focused on Paige. On Beau. On keeping it together while we're here in this horrible in-between space. I haven't let myself think of what I lost. The phone feels too slick in my hands. Too nice. I'd trade it to have my photo back. "I lost the photo, the only one I had."

"The one of your dad?" he asks, his voice gentle. He knows what that photo means to me. What it meant to me, before it became a curl of scrap paper in a pile of debris.

"I didn't have time to get anything out."

Beau was in my bed that night. We were in my room. I could have grabbed the photo on the way out, but I didn't. I could have grabbed my wallet, but I didn't. I inhaled smoke and we left. I always thought, if I woke up in a fire, I'd have the presence of mind to take the only evidence of my dad with me. I was wrong. When the house is on fire like that, you don't think. You just run.

"I'm sorry, Janie."

"It's not just that. It's everything. My wallet. I don't even have ID anymore." Frustration feels better than grief. It can at least cover it up for a minute. "It's a whole process to prove who you are. It's like I'm nobody. I can't prove who I am without proof of who I am. And I'm not sure who to trust around here, since whoever set the fire—"

Noah curses again. Hot embarrassment flashes over my cheeks. Cold dread in the pit of my stomach.

"Noah, don't—"

"You have to be fucking kidding me." His voice has dropped low, the anger not concealed at all. It's only pitched to avoid detection by overzealous foster parents who don't care for emotions. It shakes me to the core. "Somebody tried to get to you?"

"It's not like—"

"And what was that rich asshole doing, Jane? Was he doing anything to protect you?"

Tears slip down over my cheeks. My hand trembles around the too-good phone. "It wasn't his fault. Don't be mad at him. Or me. It wasn't anyone's fault."

It was someone's fault. Someone set the fire. Part of me wants to accept some of the blame. Did I piss someone off from Beau's past?

Noah lets out a breath on the other end of the line. "I'm sorry. I'm sorry. But you get why I have to come out there. It's not safe out there. These people with money get themselves in over their heads. They don't care who they put at risk in the process. It's a trap."

"You don't—there's no need to come out here. I'm fine."

"You're not fine. You're crying. You don't have any of your stuff, that damn house burned down..." Another deep breath. He's barely in control of himself. He's started pacing again. His footsteps echo on the sidewalk. I can't picture where he's at. Not very long ago, I'd have asked him where he was. Now it'll only make me feel worse to imagine Noah walking alone on a street I used to know. "You need to come home."

The word *home* makes me flinch away from the phone like he's yelled into it. Where is home for me? Not Houston. Not anymore. Not this inn, either.

I thought I didn't belong anywhere before the fire. Now it's even more true.

I have none of the touchstones to remind me of who I am.

Of who I'm supposed to be.

Everything has been burned up and tossed around in the fire. I came here because I had a clear goal in mind. Do the job. Get the money. Go to college, become a social worker, and break the cycle that brought me here in the first place, alone and more than a little desperate for well-paying work.

None of this has played out the way I thought. I didn't expect to love Paige as much as I do. I didn't expect to fall for my boss. And for all of it to go up in smoke—

"I don't know. Maybe I will." He knows me. He's seen me at my worst. On my darkest, most horrible days. It's tempting to believe that Noah has the answers to the constant storm in my mind. Years ago, when I first met him in the foster home, I was sad about leaving my last place. He comforted me. *People like you and me, we don't stay in one place for long. If you leave early enough, you won't miss them when you're gone.* "Maybe it's a sign that I should come home. I really thought it was safe here."

How could it have turned out to be less safe than a lifetime in foster homes? Every new address was another roll of the dice. I was supposed to have a better chance here.

"Come home," he says again, and I want to give in. It hurts to think about giving in. It's painful to imagine the scene with Paige. She might fold her little arms over her chest and turn her back on me, stone-faced and silent. Or she might break down with her red face and her frantic screaming. How can I walk away from that? I promised her I'd stay. I made a promise to her.

It feels like the two sides of my heart are being tugged apart by strong hands. Noah's waiting on one side, and Paige and Beau on the other. A sob wrenches out of me. "Noah, I—"

"Just come home. We can figure things out when you get here. You don't have to think about it. Just buy a plane ticket back to Houston."

The alarm on my phone rings, cutting through our conversation. I have it set for eight o'clock every morning, though Paige usually comes and finds me before then.

I'm on the clock.

"I have to go," I tell Noah.

"No. Jane. We need to talk about this. Don't hang up. Don't—"

I end the call and put the phone in my pocket, then go to find Paige.

She isn't there. Her bed is empty. The door to her bathroom stands open, the small room dark inside. She's not in her room, or Beau's, or any of the other guest rooms.

I wipe away my tears with the hem of my shirt. My heart thumps with renewed fear at the absence of her. What if she's wandered away? *Oh, no.*

We're in a new place. You know how she likes to

hide.

She's not on the upper floor. I check every room and the linen closet. The only access to the attic is via a pull-down staircase, so she can't be up there. One of my feet slips on the stairs going down to the first floor, but I catch myself on the railing.

Not in the kitchen. Not in the living room. "Paige?"

No answer.

The inn has a finished basement, and I hesitate between looking outside and looking down there. Out or down? God, I don't know. I have to do both, so I rush down the stairs at top speed. It's cool and still down here. The sparse furniture is taken care of, like everything in the inn, but it's not a space we've used.

She's not in the main room, with its two couches and shelves stacked with board games.

I'm about to give up, to sprint upstairs and search the beach for her, when I hear the sniffle from the laundry room.

Next to the industrial washer and dryer is the exit for the laundry chute, covered by a door that can be pulled back with a knob. It's open an inch.

I can see Paige's toes through the crack.

She goes absolutely still when I pull open the

door. Paige looks stricken in the dim light coming through a window high on the ceiling. Her cheeks are red. If she's about to have another meltdown, I can handle it, but this feels different. I open my arms wide to her and back up a few steps to give her space.

"Come here, sweetheart."

She hesitates for a painful few seconds. But then she scrambles out of the laundry chute and launches herself at me.

I go down to the floor with her and lean against the opposite wall. She rests her head on my chest, breathing hard.

Paige relaxes a little when I put my arms around her and lean us back on the pillows. I run my fingers through her hair, working out the little tangles that have accumulated over the course of the morning. I don't say anything. Sometimes it's better to nudge a person when they're upset. Sometimes it's better to keep your mouth shut. At least staying quiet gives me a chance to collect myself.

Paige takes a shuddering breath. "I don't want to die."

Oh, it hurts to hear those words in her voice. She shouldn't be thinking about death this young, but she can't help it. Her parents are dead.

"You're going to live a long, long time," I promise her, even though I can't promise it.

"Okay, but I don't want you to die." The quaver in her voice almost makes tears spill over again, but I'm not going to break down. She's experienced too much loss already, and now she's even more afraid. It's awful. I have to be strong for her.

"I'm not planning to die anytime soon." This is the truth, at least. I'm not planning on it. Right now I'm planning to live forever if it'll mean making her feel better. I run a hand over her back. "Are you worried about it?"

"Yes," she says in a small voice. "If you and Beau die, who will take care of me?"

A truly impossible question. I don't know what Beau's will says, but if he dies, it wouldn't be me. I would go back to Houston, and I would once again become no one. "Someone will always be here to take care of you. But we're both going to live a long time. Until you're a grown-up."

A pause. The wheels are going to come off my answers pretty soon if she keeps this up. I really will cry. I don't know how to explain the process of finding your own stand-ins for family. It wouldn't be comforting to her.

"When I'm grown up," Paige says, "can I still

play at the beach?"

"Yes, of course." Sweet relief. "You don't have to wait until then. Should we play at the beach this afternoon?"

"Sand castles," says Paige. "I want to make the towers."

"I'll make the walls."

"Not too close to the water." She takes a big breath and lets it out. "I don't want the waves to knock it down before we're done."

"Not too close," I agree.

It gets quiet between us again, and I smooth down her hair. Playing Monopoly with Beau and Paige yesterday felt like this. That's what it would be like to have a family. She still hasn't lifted her head from my chest. This is what it would be like to have a daughter. All these difficult, painful moments with impossible questions tucked in next to the sweet, innocent ones.

"Do you think she'll come back?" Paige asks.

"Who?"

"The woman on the cliff. The one wearing the nightgown. She used to walk outside our old house, before it burned down."

CHAPTER SEVENTEEN

Beau Rochester

NOW THAT THE former Coach House is no longer a crime scene, I'm forced to deal with the insurance company. I could just pay to have it replaced myself, but it's complicated because the house is technically in the trust that's in place for Paige. Then I deal with the contractors. I want the house rebuilt so I can get Jane and Paige somewhere that doesn't feel so exposed. At the very least, I want the accusing rubble cleared off the cliff.

Phone calls eat up most of the afternoon while Jane and Paige are at the beach. The whole damn thing is an exercise in frustration. I hate sitting so long for phone calls, but my leg throbs when I stand or pace. The two of them come back from the beach with sun-pink cheeks. Jane's quiet at dinner. The shadows in her eyes eat at me.

I want her alone in a room so I can back her against the wall and write questions on her skin. She'll give me the answers. They just have to be coaxed out of her. We put Paige to bed, dancing around the worry she won't talk about.

Jane slips into my bedroom a few minutes after Paige has fallen asleep. I'm at the dresser, pulling a sweater over my head.

From the shift in the air, I think she might be crying. There's a certain relief in that. I can hold her too close. I can wipe her tears away.

Taste them on her lips.

But when I turn to face her, she's not crying. Jane clasps her hands in front of her, and there's pained indecision on her face.

"What is it? What's wrong?"

"This might sound—" She shakes her head. "Last night, while I was giving Paige her bath, I saw this woman walking on the beach. She was there one second, and then just… gone."

"Probably Marjorie out for a walk."

"In a white nightgown? With blonde hair?"

It's like she's tipped an ice pitcher down into my gut. "Not Marjorie, then." She's a redhead. "A guest from one of the other bed-and-breakfasts, Jane. People walk on the beach."

"That's the thing." More color fades from her

cheeks. "Paige mentioned a woman this morning. She said a woman used to walk on the cliff by the house before it burned down." Jane swallows. "She said the woman wore a white nightgown, too."

Fuck.

I want to back away from her, but there's no space left in the room to do it. The window's the only illusion of escape. An empty stretch of sand waits in front of rippling waves. Makes it hard to see if there's anything in the water. I can't logic my way out of this. It would be easy to dismiss them both. Chalk it up to being tired and stressed.

My stomach turns.

Jane touches my elbow, her fingertips light on the fabric. I feel like a house fire waiting to start. Her dark eyes find mine. "What should we do?"

She's urgent. Afraid. I want to soothe her, not scare her.

But she *should* be afraid. My heart pumps pure adrenaline into my veins. I've already installed a security system. There's not much more I can do to protect the house other than hiring armed guards to stand around a mostly-empty beach.

What would that say about my sanity, if I

surrounded this place with mercenaries? What would it do to Jane's sanity? To Paige's? It would only be confirmation that we're not safe. Visible, unavoidable confirmation.

Then again, maybe we're not safe. It might only confirm the truth.

Her voice trembles. "Who could be doing this?"

If the sightings on the beach are related, then it's a blonde woman. "It could be Zoey Aldridge. I thought of her from the beginning, but she has an alibi. The cops already checked her out. But there's always a chance she manufactured it."

"What can we do about it?"

"I'll keep pushing the detectives in her direction. Unfortunately it's a small department. It would be easy for her to produce a fake charter for her jet."

"Do you really think it's her?"

"I don't know, but it works. Zoey has a reason to hate me."

"Because you… stopped dating her?"

"I never started dating her, not really." At Jane's disbelieving look, I elaborate. "We went out a couple times in LA. She wanted more. I didn't. She kept texting me all the damn time, even when I completely ghosted her. There were red flags all over the place."

"Then why did you call her?"

"Because I was getting too close to you," I admit, my tone grim. "You were getting too close to me. And I thought that bringing in a third party, a woman who would sweep in and make assumptions, might somehow stop the inevitable."

The look she gives me is pure wounded pride. "That is so messed up."

"Yes. I did warn you about me."

"But if she has a history of acting out, then she should be at the top of the suspect list."

"Joe Causey doesn't give a shit what I say. He's determined to pin this on me somehow. But it may come down to that. I'll go to jail for insurance fraud and be done with it."

"Why?" she breathes. "Why does Joe Causey hate you so much over some childhood issue?"

"Because it's not just a childhood issue. He's Emily's brother."

Jane's mouth drops open. She actually takes a step back, putting space between us. Good. Good. She's finally realizing where the danger is here. It's me, and all these tangles from the past. "What?"

"Yeah. He blames me for her death. And for her ending up with Rhys."

Two spots of color have appeared on her

cheeks. Her hand goes to her throat. "That means he's Paige's uncle."

"Yes. He fought me for custody." Family court is hell on earth. It reeks of small-town gossip and old vendettas. Everything hinges on the mood of the judge, who pretends to be impartial in his black robe and spends every Wednesday night at a card game with the mayor and the principal of the school. He's always liked Joe. "But Emily named me in her will, which probably took him by surprise. It took me by surprise. She loved her brother. Spoiled him, actually. Was very protective of him. No one was more surprised than me to find out she'd named me. The judge had the ultimate decision, but based on her wishes, he granted me custody."

Jane's eyes soften, her brow furrowed. I don't know what kind of calculations she does in moments like this. They probably have more to do with how good she is, how innocent, than the ones I make. "We have to tell the police about the woman on the beach."

"He's a bastard and a bully."

Her chin comes up a little bit. "I know you don't trust him, but he's the only chance we have of catching whoever did this. Because I think they're still doing it. I think they're still following us."

"You know what the fire chief said to me? No. Nevermind."

"Tell me." Her eyes bore into me. "I deserve the truth, remember."

Yes, she deserves that much from me. More, really. "You'll think I'm crazy if I tell you. Even I think I'm crazy." I feel crazy now. Like the beam did more than fuck up my knee and trap me in a burning building. Like it knocked something loose in my mind. The beam's just an excuse, though. I've had this recurring suspicion for months. Since the accident.

"What is it?"

Jane's so sweet. So hopeful. She's a goddamn miracle, is what she is. The kind of like she's lived—so rough and so painful. It shouldn't have let her trust me. It shouldn't give her big dark eyes that look up at me like I have any of the answers. Like I could keep her safe, if only she can solve this one problem. "What if Emily survived?"

Her face pales. "Emily like Paige's mom? Emily Rochester?"

"I don't know. Yes." I look over the beach again. Nothing but empty sand. No woman in a white nightgown. The visual is creepy as hell. A nightgown on the cliffside? A nightgown on the beach? "She had blonde curls like that. And I keep having this feeling of dread. Like somebody's watching."

Eyes on the back of my neck. Not just at the house. Here, too.

"Did you tell this to the police?" she asks.

"Christ. Of course not. They're looking for a real person. Not a ghost." I look away from her like a coward. The sincerity in her eyes is too much to see right now. My heart punches faster. "I haven't been calling the cops. The opposite. I've been avoiding them. Causey's demanding an interview with Paige. My lawyer has managed to put him off so far because she needs time to recover, but he's insisting. We're going to have to let him. And—" Among all those phone calls with the insurance company today, there was another one. Joe Causey's demand on my voicemail. "He wants to interview you again."

Emotions flash through her dark eyes. Dread. And then a beautiful resolve. "Okay."

"I don't want him near Paige. I don't want him near you."

"We might be the only ones," she says.

The only ones in the world. The only ones left. When that fire was coming down around us, we were the only ones in the world. Jane's face was the last thing I was going to see before I died. Jane, dying herself, for love of me. She'd accepted it. Her death. But I couldn't. I couldn't accept a damn thing when it came to her. Not the way I felt. Not the way I wanted her. It didn't matter, in the end, whether I accepted it or not. Hasn't changed anything.

I want her, and it's not good for her. None of this is good for her.

It's dangerous.

"The only witnesses," she continues. "We might be the only witnesses who can place this person at the house, and out on the beach. Paige and I."

My veins burn with how much I hate this. How much I hate the thought of letting Joe sit across a table from Paige or Jane. I don't want his eyes on them, or his questions in their memories. I don't want his twisted suggestions of guilt to get under their skin, or under mine. But if they're right, and there's someone out here, someone following us...

What other choice do I have? I can't hold him off forever. And I can't pack us up and disappear into the night. Paige wouldn't be able to handle it.

"I wish you would stop."

Jane's dark eyes are luminous in the lamp from my bedside table. She has both arms crossed in front of her stomach. A shield. "Stop what?"

"Stop holding yourself so far away. It's like you're gone, and we're in the same room." She takes a shaky breath. "You're not protecting me from anything when you do that."

"I'm not protecting you from anything, ever." There's a person on the beach. A person on the cliff. Someone lit a fire above our heads. Joe Causey's breathing down our necks.

I can't make it stop.

"Not standing over there, you're not."

I do what I've wanted to do since she came in the room. Two steps and she's close enough to crush her to my body. Jane sighs, like this is a good thing, like this is an improvement and not a faulty lifeboat off a sinking ship. She smells like the shampoo from the inn and sunscreen from their afternoon at the beach. It's an innocent scent.

"I promised myself I wouldn't touch you again," I want to lick it off her. Inhale it until there's nothing left. With her body against mine like this, I want to make her a hundred promises. I want to tell her not to worry. The urge is so strong I almost say it. *Don't worry, Jane. I'll fix everything.* But I'm failing miserably. My love is dangerous, but it's fucking unstoppable.

"I saw her," she says against my chest, and I hear the tiniest waver in her voice. Like she's sure I won't believe her. I'm sure she got by in her previous life by keeping her mouth shut. I know it from the way her arms hold tight around my waist.

I don't want to have to do this to her. Sit her in that room across from Joe Causey and let him disbelief her. But it's coming. The only thing I can do is try to gain a little control over where it happens, and when.

"I believe you," I tell her. Jane squeezes tighter. "We'll make this quick. It'll be over soon."

CHAPTER EIGHTEEN

Jane Mendoza

IT TAKES A couple days of negotiation between lawyers and the police department, but finally it's agreed that Joe Causey will come here. It took a while but still feels too soon.

Paige goes first, red-faced and silent, her arms crossed over her chest. I wish I could be in there for moral support, but apparently it's important that we're questioned separately. At least Beau is inside with her, but that presents its own kind of danger.

He's volatile when he's near the detective.

I can't think over the heavy beat of my heart. The sharp edge of Joe's voice is all I can hear through the floor. Pacing is too loud but standing still is its own form of torture.

I'm braced for the yelling of men or the screams of a scared child.

They never come.

"Jane?" Mateo stands at the foot of the stairs, Paige a foot away from him with her jaw jutted out. I go to meet them with a racing pulse. Sweat pricks at my hairline. I don't trust the police. It feels awful having Joe in this house. "They're ready for you."

At the bottom of the steps, I get down on one knee to look Paige in the eye. "How are you doing, sweetheart? Can I give you a hug?"

She gives a quick shake of her head. No. That's fair. I suppose it mirrors how I feel about this, too. No. Not now, not today, not ever. But like her, I don't have a choice about it.

"How about we go get some ice cream at the shop downtown?" Mateo suggests.

Paige cuts a glance up at him. It'll be better if she's not here for whatever happens next. Better for her to be away from the thick tension in the house.

I'm torn between not wanting to let her out of my sight and not wanting her to be here while I'm being questioned. Interviewed. Interrogated.

Whatever you call it when you're not a suspect...

But maybe I am a suspect.

"You can get extra chocolate syrup," I tell her.

"And all the sprinkles you want. We'll be waiting for you when you get home. I'll wait on the front porch."

"Do you promise?" she whispers, barely audible.

"I swear." A small part of me thinks something big might happen. Joe Causey might announce that they have proof I'm responsible for the fire. He might arrest me before she gets back. No, that's crazy. "Right by the door. I'll be waiting when you get back."

Paige hesitates, and so does my heart. I can't walk away from her if she melts down. And I can't hold her on my lap while I face Joe Causey.

"Okay." She takes a tiny step toward Mateo.

He lets out a breath. "Extra chocolate syrup it is."

"And sprinkles," I hear her reminding him, her voice only a shadow of its usual strength.

They leave the inn, and I have no choice but to go into the room.

A rectangular table sits in the middle of the room, pulled away from the wall where it normally rests. It's innocuous, usually. A place to play the chess game that normally sits there. Somewhere to set down a cup of tea while you read a book.

Now it's become the center of the room with chairs on either side.

It's a dark-stained wood instead of stainless steel, but I can still imagine it as an interrogation room. Especially with Joe Causey giving me a cool, assessing look over the surface.

"Good afternoon, Ms. Mendoza," he says with fake politeness.

Or maybe it's real politeness. Maybe I'm overly suspicious because of all the cops I saw dragging children out of their family homes, taking them away from the mothers who were working the only jobs they could, stripping or prostituting themselves or selling drugs, to feed their children. And then the irony is, the government would give money to the foster parents. They wouldn't help an actual family stay together, but they'd supplement some random alcoholic's liquor fund if he had a spare bedroom. What kind of system was that?

I saw cops take sixteen-year-olds to jail when what they really needed was a hot meal and a mentor. I saw cops shoot foster kids in the street for doing nothing at all while rich kids were on TV getting off on theft and manslaughter.

Logically I know that some cops are good, but the problem is that when you're faced with one of them, there's no way to tell whether this is one of the good ones or not.

"Hello," I say, my tone wary. I stand at the door.

The first man I notice is Edward Basil, the lawyer who showed up this morning. He has a fatherly air and kind eyes. He sat with me for a few minutes before Causey arrived. *Just tell the truth. If you don't remember something, say you don't remember. If he asks you questions quickly, you can take as much time as you need to answer. He'll want it to seem like he's in charge, but really you run the show, Jane.*

It was a nice sentiment, even if I can't quite believe it.

Beau pulls out a chair for me. In his eyes I find reassurance and a sense of belonging. He may be Paige's uncle, Paige's guardian, but he's my boss. He'll protect me from this—whatever this is. "This shouldn't take too long," he says in a warning tone directed at the detectives.

Only then do I notice the other detective in the room. A woman with short blonde hair and a pinstripe pantsuit watches us. "Of course we don't want to inconvenience you," she says, her soothing tone a sharp counterpoint to Joe Causey's dark gaze. She gives me a small, professional smile. "I'm Detective Nell Moss, and I believe you've met my partner, Detective Joe Causey."

Maybe it's a good cop/bad cop setup.

I slide into the seat that Beau holds out for me and place my hands on the table. That feels weird, so I shove them onto my lap instead. I can't help but imagine bright lights on my face and cinder block walls. A camera recording my every move in the corner. And a one-way mirror where a prosecutor watches, ready to press charges. I know the inn is comfortable, cozy, but I can feel none of its warmth as the cops take seats opposite me.

"Can you state your name for the record?" the woman asks.

"Jane Elizabeth Mendoza."

The female detective writes it down on an old-fashioned flip notepad. "You understand that you are not under arrest. Your answers here are given of your own free will, and they are true to the best of your ability."

Hearing the words *under arrest* from a detective makes my pulse pound. I glance at the lawyer. He gives an encouraging nod, adding, "You're not under oath," he says gently, with a sideways look at the detectives. "And there's no reason to suspect her of anything."

Joe Causey leans forward. "I wouldn't go that far. You're not under arrest. Not under oath. Only because we don't have enough evidence to hold you."

"If you badger my client, I will terminate this interview," the lawyer says, his voice stern.

Beau tenses, every muscle coiled for defense. Or attack.

It should make me feel safer, but instead it makes me feel more afraid—as if I'm stuck in a battle between wolves and bears, as if I'm a mouse destined to be ripped apart by both sides.

Detective Moss clears her throat. "We understand you witnessed someone walking on the beach. Can you tell me about that?"

The way she says it is nice... but a little condescending. As if she thinks I'm making a big deal about a tourist on the beach. "Maybe it's nothing," I say, my voice halting, hesitating. "I'm a little nervous after the fire. A little jumpy."

"You're fine," Beau says, his voice hard. "The detectives requested this meeting."

Right. They requested this meeting. I sit a little taller in the chair and lift my chin. It's not easy for me to face them, but I'm determined to do it with my head held high. "I was giving Paige a bath. She likes to take her time, so it's a full hour of splash time. I usually try to give her her privacy while also making sure she's safe, so I check into the bathroom and also spend some time in the bedroom with the door open. I fold laundry and get her clothes ready while I wait."

I take a breath and glance at the lawyer for reassurance. He nods at me to continue.

"That night I looked out the window. There was a woman walking on the sand. I had the impression of blonde hair the way the moonlight reflected it. But the strange part was that she was wearing this long, white nightgown. It seemed out of place on the beach."

"Did she do anything suspicious?" This from Detective Causey.

My skin prickles the way it did when I saw her.

The truth is she wasn't necessarily being suspicious, but somehow my instincts warned me that this wasn't right. It warned me that this wasn't... safe.

"No, I just thought it was odd. I'm used to couples walking together or someone walking a dog. Then I checked on Paige, and when I looked back, she was gone."

"A white nightgown," Detective Moss says, her pen poised to write more.

"It was far away, but it seemed like something long. It went past her feet." I don't share that it looked like she was floating along the beach. I don't think they'd receive that information well. I'd probably get locked up in an insane asylum. "And it was long sleeved."

"Even though it's summer," Detective Moss murmurs.

The truth is the nights here are still just as cold as the winter nights in Houston. But I've learned that people here consider anything short of a deep freeze to be temperate weather. At least I arrived in the early spring, when the snow had passed. The only thing I faced was freezing rain.

"Did you mention her to Rochester?" This from Causey.

"No," I say, my cheeks burning as I remember what happened when he showed up.

Tell me the truth. Trust me with it. He'd given me more than words in those scalding moments. He'd touched me. Tasted me. Made me gasp and pant with desire before pulling back. His words had doused the embers in a single instant.

Someone was in the house that night. Someone lit a goddamn match.

"I didn't think it was important," I say. "Not until Paige told me about seeing a woman wearing a nightgown on the cliffside, near the Coach House. It was strange enough to see it in one place... but in two different places? It seemed suspicious."

Detective Causey gives me a cold smile. "That, Ms. Rochester, is what we in the law enforcement profession call circumstantial. It means nothing."

My cheeks heat. "My last name is Mendoza."

"Oh," Causey says with fake apology. "Of course you're still Ms. Mendoza. He hasn't coughed up an engagement ring yet, has he?"

Rochester glares at him, but I don't want him to say anything. I don't want him to defend me. Not when I can defend myself.

I spread my hands on the table as if to say, *what's next?* "If it's circumstantial, then why are you asking me about it? Do you have some questions that *are* relevant?"

Challenge sparks in Causey's blue eyes. "Here's something directly relevant to the fire. Do you know that Rochester changed his will?"

I glance at Beau, but he's tense now. And silent.

"No," I say. "It's none of my business."

Detective Moss studies me intently, as if she's trying to look right through me. To the very broken heart of me. "Actually it has quite a bit to do with you. Only a few days before the fire Beau Rochester added an addendum to his will granting you a large sum of money when he died. You stood to become a billionaire if he died in that fire."

Something tightens around my throat. He did that? Why would he do that? Why wouldn't he tell me? I look at him. "Is that true?" I whisper.

He doesn't meet my gaze. He's busy glaring at Causey. "I told you she saved my goddamn life."

Detective Causey makes a show of checking some notes. "As I understand it, the firefighters saved your life. Ms. Mendoza was in the house with you, that's true. Perhaps she was only making sure that you couldn't escape."

Horror streaks through my veins. What if Beau believes that? I look at him, but he's furious. I'm no longer worried about him suspecting me of anything, but now I'm worried for a different reason. He looks a hairbreadth away from launching himself across the table. This may not be a real interrogation room, but I'm sure assaulting a police officer won't go over well in any setting.

"Goddamn it," Beau says. "I told you to look at Zoey Aldridge."

"We did," Detective Moss says, looking serious.

"He doesn't give a shit," Beau says. "Causey isn't checking any leads."

Detective Moss doesn't even deny it. "I checked out the lead. Thoroughly. I flew out to LA. Found footage from clubs and restaurants that prove she was in the city."

Causey grins. "Lost your scapegoat, didn't you?"

Something passes over Beau's expression. Something venomous. "Hell, maybe we've been looking at the wrong people all this time. Women. Always blaming the women, but the person who wants to hurt me the most—it's you."

"You think so?" Causey says, a touch of mocking in his voice. "Where's your evidence?"

"Ignore him," I say, touching Beau's arm. He's vibrating with coiled menace, his muscles bunched. "He's just trying to scare us. Don't let him get to you."

Causey glances at where we're touching. "Is that how you got him to make you a beneficiary? It definitely worked. How many times did you have to sleep with him? Once for every billion? You must have a nice pussy to go for that much."

Beau launches himself across the table. He's

stopped short by the lawyer, who's surprisingly fast for his gray hair and genial demeanor. He leans across the table, catching Beau before he can assault a police officer. "Don't," he says, breathing hard. Then he turns to the detectives. "Did we mention we've been recording the interview? I think the police chief will have something to say about the way you just spoke to a witness."

Causey was looking smug when Beau reacted to his taunts, but now he turns red. "You were recording us without consent? That's illegal."

"Don't threaten me," the lawyer says, low and fierce. He's transformed into someone intimidating, and I see now why Beau hired him. "We had the consent of at least one person taking part in the communication. In addition, the conversation was audible by normal, unaided hearing. And on top of that, there was a notice that you might be recorded posted at the entrance of the inn. Or did you not read the fine print, Detective?"

Causey glares at the lawyer. Then at Beau. Then his dark, accusing gaze turns on me. His eyes remain focused on me even though his words are meant for someone else. "If she's worth so much to you, Beau, you should take better care of her."

Beau lets out a growl. "Leave her the hell

alone. I know you're only threatening her to get back at me, because you're a goddamn bully. I'm the one you want."

Causey gives him a half smile. "Don't blame me. You gave her the biggest motive in the world. And she was in the house. And like the fire chief said, she's a woman. It's only a matter of time until we find one more link. Only a matter of time until we get an arrest warrant."

CHAPTER NINETEEN

Jane Mendoza

I'M PACING IN my bedroom, unable to calm down. I'm breathing hard, sweating, freaking out so bad I'm seeing rainbow colors instead of the calm, quiet room around me.

Beau bursts through the door, his expression dark as a storm cloud.

"I didn't set the fire," I say, breathless, shaking. "I swear to you. I would never do anything to hurt you, and God, I would never hurt Paige."

He reaches behind him and shoves the door closed with his palm flat. The *thud* penetrates even my frantic, panic-drenched mind. "I know you didn't set the fucking fire," he grinds out. "This is the way Causey's trying to get to me. Through you."

"I didn't have anything to do with it, and I didn't even know about the will and—why did you do that, Beau? Why did you change your will?"

Both hands on my shoulders, his grip as intense as his expression. It's hard, almost bruising, but I wouldn't want him to go softer. This isn't a moment for gentleness. "I wanted you to have it. The money. What the hell good is the money if it can't make your life easier? If it can't send you to college? If it can't give you everything you dream about?"

I don't dream about money. I'm not dreaming about anything right now. I'm nerves and fear in a body that's out of my control. They keep accusing me of things I didn't do, and I can't stop it.

I don't want to stop Beau.

"Give me this," I tell him. I'm not even sure what I'm asking for. More. More of his intensity and his storm. Let it break over me. My teeth chatter with the adrenaline rush. I need his rough control to meet whatever this whirlwind is. "Please."

His dark eyes widen. "Tell me what you mean. Tell me exactly, Jane."

"I need—" I don't have the words for it. I can only feel it there under his skin. Coiled and waiting. As hard and possessive as he is, with his big hands on my shoulders and his body generating heat in the room.

"I don't want to think anymore. *Please.*"

I don't have answers. I didn't have them downstairs, and I don't have them now.

He must see it in my face.

"Fuck," he says, expression even darker. A raincloud about to tear open and pour. The ocean about to crash on shore. He takes my face in both his hands and pulls me into a kiss that's harder than any we've shared before. He tastes like salt and fury. Like the metallic aftertaste of a lightning strike.

The kiss is so all-consuming that it pulls my body into a new response. I was shaking before out of terror. Out of panic from that interview. Now it's pure need.

I don't need what he can give me.

I need what he can take.

All these roiling thoughts. All this fear. He can take it.

"You want me?" he asks, walking toward me. I'm forced to back up, back up, back up, until the wall stops me. It's cool and impersonal, that wall, keeping me flush against Beau's hard body. He grips my chin. His thumb runs over my trembling lips. "You want me in your mouth? Lick me? Suck me with this pretty little mouth?"

Words have escaped me. They've flown right out of my head, leaving only sensation. The sensual, ticklish feeling of his touch on my lips. The iron length of his erection against my stomach. I can't answer him with words.

Instead I flick my tongue out against his thumbpad.

His eyes turn midnight black. It's a threat, that color. The kind of night when the wind kicks up, making one-hundred-year old trees sway in the wind. There's not a single star in his sky. "Get on your knees," he says, his voice low and velvet.

For a moment I think he means he'll step back. He doesn't move. His thumb taps once, twice, three times on my lips, and I understand he means for me to slide down the wall. My knees hit the floor. He rests his hand on the wall above me, looking down, eyes glittering.

"Your leg," I manage to say, my concern for him overriding my lust.

"I'll survive," he says, a mocking half-smile on his face. "Go on."

I reach up and fumble at his belt. My fingers feel thick under this haze of arousal. Clumsy. I finally manage to open the buckle. Then I work the zipper of his jeans down over a rock-hard arousal. It's difficult at first, the denim stretched taut, and then fast the rest of the way down. There's still a layer of black fabric shielding my view.

His words come back to me in a rush. *I only wear boxer briefs. Boxers are too loose. Briefs are too tight. Boxer briefs are perfect.* He'd been teasing me, offering me that superficial intimacy, but now it strikes me as deeply personal knowledge—that I know what he prefers to wear. That I'm touching it, curling my fingers over the top, pulling the elastic down.

His cock springs out, heavy and almost painfully hot against the back of my hand. It leaves a streak of precum painted across my wrist.

I grasp him in my fist and glance up at him. His teeth are gritted. It looks like pain, but I know it's something else. It's that singular ache I feel between my legs, wanting so much it hurts.

This close, in the tiny pocket of universe between him and the wall, all I can see is his cock. All I can smell is his salt-musk. I place a hesitant kiss on the side of his erection.

It jumps in my hand, startling me.

"Don't play with me," he says, his voice low.

He's never been this way with me, this intense, this severe. I should be afraid, but somehow it emboldens me. I've brought him to this pitch. "Or else what?"

"Or else you're going to get fucked."

A shiver runs through me, even though I don't fully understand the warning. I thought that's what we were doing here.

Then he pulls from my hand. He fists his own cock, fucking himself.

"Open," he says, and now I understand.

He's not going to let me suck him. I won't be able to lick or kiss. I won't be able to play with him. Instead I'll be given his cock. I open my lips, and he pushes forward. My mouth is flooded with salt, with arousal. I'm full, gasping, almost gagging, and then he pulls back.

"Again," he murmurs. That's the only warning I get, the split second of knowledge before I'm filled again, my eyes watering with the pressure against my throat, tears running down my cheeks. He holds longer inside my mouth. When he pulls out, I'm gasping for air.

"Again."

This time it goes too far. My throat convulses around him. My hands fly up, without thinking about it, without planning. I don't want to stop him necessarily, but my body reacts. I try to pull back but the wall blocks me. My hands push at his thighs. It's like trying to move a brick wall.

He pulls back, looking down at me, shaking his head. "No, ma'am."

His tone is gently admonishing, playful and serious at the same time. It's humiliating for him to chastise me this way, but my body reacts as if he swiped a finger across my clit. I'm immediately hotter, wetter. My thighs clench together.

"Give me your hands," he says.

I lift them, and he pins my wrists to the wall on either side of my head. Then he pushes forward again. His progress is slow but inexorable. I try to open wide, to submit to him. *Don't fight, don't fight.* There's a moment of panic, but he mutters words of praise and encouragement.

"Breathe through your nose." The words are like a low, almost inaudible music in the room. "Relax. You can do this, sweetheart. You can take me."

Tears run down my cheeks. I feel them drip off my chin and fall onto my chest. He holds himself inside my throat. I swallow around him convulsively, again and again. My lungs burn without air. A circle of darkness closes. Then he pulls out and air fills me up, almost violent in its return.

"Or maybe I won't survive," he mutters, his

midnight eyes glinting down at me.

A hand fists in my hair. He uses it as a handle to lift me up off the floor, up and up and up until he can kiss me again. His teeth rake along my bottom lip—a flash of pain—and then he's stripping me down. Fast. Efficient.

My shirt comes over my head. My yoga pants. Nothing withstands him.

"More," he says. Nothing else. Just *more*. He's going to take more.

"Yes," I breathe. Take me. Take everything.

He's breathing harder as he skims his hands over my shoulders, my breasts. This is as sweet as he's willing to be right now. As slow as he's willing to go.

I don't want him to be careful with me.

He's not.

He moves us over to my bed, turns me to face him, and pushes me up onto the mattress. There's no hesitation now. He moves me how he wants me, and oh, God, it's such a relief.

Finally, finally. I don't have to think. I can just feel.

He spreads my legs apart, arranging me however he wants. And he wants me open.

Two fingers tease at my entrance. It's like he's testing how wet I am. How swollen. How ready.

Then he shoves two fingers inside, fast, unrelenting, and my whole body bows with shock. Even as aroused as I am, it still feels like too much.

He kneels beside me, leaning over me. I feel dominated, whether I'm against the wall or against the bed. It's my own personal cliff. He walks me to the edge, then pushes me over.

He finds a spot inside me that makes me gasp.

"What are you doing?" I manage to pant.

"Writing you a message," he says, sensual knowledge in his eyes. He knows exactly how he's making me feel, how hard it is to stay still.

He's written on different parts of me—my arm, my stomach. Drawing letters that spell out secret words. This is the first time he's written inside me, his fingers stroking over a sensitive place, making me squirm and beg. "Please, please, please."

"Wait until I'm finished," he admonishes. "Or you won't get your reward."

"What are you writing?"

His fingers work inside, deft and merciless. "Pay attention. You tell me. You have to tell me what it says if you want me to let you come."

"Nooo," I moan, moving my hips, restless and hungry.

The message marches forward, letter by letter,

an exquisite torture. It drives me closer to climax. I'm nearing the edge, fighting it. My heels dig into the bed as if I can stop the tumble. Then he finishes the last letter with a swirling flourish deep inside.

I come so hard my vision turns as black as his eyes.

Before I can fully recover, he flips me over so I'm face down. My body's made of liquid, heavy with salt like the ocean, frothy and indistinct at the edges. His hands cover mine as he places them on the headboard. Those same palms on my hips, hauling them back to the angle he wants them. He spreads my thighs. I can't catch my breath.

"Hold on," he says.

I expect him to take me then. Brace for it, even.

Instead I'm met with the flat of his tongue along my center. Wet, rough, heat. It's so different from what I was expecting that I come on his tongue instantly. He groans at the taste. The sound turns off the part of me that was thinking at all anymore.

Then he's up on his knees behind me. "Hold on, hold on," he says, and the thick head of him is at my opening.

He doesn't wait for me to find the right angle

or work myself over him.

He takes what he wants.

And what he wants is to be inside me to the point of stretch. To the point of ache. I don't have time to adjust to him and I don't want it. He brushes against a spot deep inside that stops my breath, and my next taste of oxygen sends me spiraling out into thoughtless, mindless pleasure.

Before I came here, I would have been embarrassed at the sounds I'm making. Animal whimpers and wordless begging. But it doesn't matter, because Beau's a match for me. He grunts in a way that reminds me of moonlit branches and carpets of moss. We aren't people right now. We've been reduced to our primal selves.

"What did you—" My voice breaks on a moan. I have to begin again. To beg for what I didn't earn, because I came when I wasn't supposed to. "What did you write before? Inside me?"

His answer is a wordless snarl.

"Please," I say, breathless. "I want to know."

"Don't leave," he says on a growl. "Don't ever leave me."

For a moment I think he's refusing to tell me, but then I realize, this is the answer. That's what he wrote inside me, fingers on my swollen, inner skin, making my orgasm.

DONTEVERLEAVEME

I come again, and his natural rhythm starts to break apart like the ocean in the middle of a storm. He fucks me like the waves crash on the beach, one after the other, fast and hard.

They don't care about upsetting pristine sand.

"This is mine," Beau says. "This. Is. Mine."

The raw possession in his voice makes me clench around him again and he curses and then he's coming too, all of him hot and hard and moving over me like I belong to him.

CHAPTER TWENTY

Jane Mendoza

THE INTERVIEW WITH Joe Causey was terrible. Horrible. But afterward, with Beau—that was something we both needed. I needed him to be that way. He needed me to be that way. Pliant. Submissive. I gave myself to him with complete and utter trust. He wasn't gentle with me. He didn't treat me like porcelain, but then I'm not fine china. I'm forged in fire.

He knew he could be rough with me.

He knew I wouldn't break.

It's early when I hear Paige's footsteps outside my room. The bed feels empty without Beau, but he doesn't feel as far away as he has. We've found a middle ground. We can do this. I push my hair back from my face and swing my legs over the side of the bed just as the doorknob turns.

"Hey," I tell her. "Are you ready for breakfast?"

She nods, blue eyes bright.

I pull on one of the crewneck sweaters Mateo brought from Nordstrom. It's meant to be casual. It's still a million times nicer than most of the dresses I've owned in my life. Still new and soft. I think it'll be this soft even when it's taken another fifty trips through the wash.

A quick change out of sleep shorts into yoga pants, and I'm ready. We make a detour on the way downstairs to brush our teeth.

Beau's door is still shut. He's been tense lately. Stressed. If he can sleep, I'll let him.

Marjorie's already in the kitchen when we come in. It's just past seven so she's getting breakfast ready. She turns away from the countertop and smiles at Paige. "I'm making waffles," she says. "Want some?"

"With extra syrup," Paige says, climbing onto one of the stools at the island.

"Of course." Marjorie winks at her, then turns back to a waffle iron perched next to the stove. "I'll have bacon and eggs along with it, and coffee's ready, too. I got this new creamer the other day that's absolutely delicious if you like hazelnut."

I'm used to drinking my coffee black, which

was always the cheapest way to have it when we could get it. There was a convenience store that Noah and I would stop at on the way home from school sometimes.

The flavored coffee was always out of our budget.

"I'd love some." Especially since my eyelids are still weighted from last night. I slept deeply, but it's early, and the last few weeks have been a lot.

I find Marjorie's new creamer in the fridge. It's a boutique brand with a sleek logo and a list of accomplishments on the front. Organic. Hand pressed. Superfood. The last one makes me raise my eyebrow, but I pour into my mug anyway.

The creamer turns the coffee a sandy color. It's probably too much, but I'm already dressed in this new life. My new phone is in the pocket of my yoga pants. There should be no guilt in enjoying expensive coffee creamer.

And it tastes really good. I must make some sound, because when I open my eyes again, Paige is making a face at me. "Coffee's gross," she says.

"Not this coffee." It's scary how easy it is to get used to the good life. How will I go back to canisters of black powder in a Mr. Coffee we picked up at a garage sale?

A thump at the front door of the inn makes Paige's eyes go wide. "What was that?"

Marjorie smiles over her shoulder at her. "The morning paper. I like to have one out for the guests. Do you want to go grab it, Paige?"

Paige scrambles down from the stool, eager to be helpful.

I lean my hip on the countertop and take another sip of coffee. God, it's good. Sun slants gently through the window over the sink. A new day. Hopefully one without Joe Causey in it.

Things did not end well with Joe yesterday, but there's nothing more I can tell the police. I doubt Beau will let them come back. We should be able to breathe.

At least for this one day.

The waffle maker dings. Marjorie tilts the fresh waffle onto a plate with a spatula. "Have any plans for the day? Weather looks gorgeous so far."

"Maybe we'll go to the beach." It's hard not to relish how easy this question is. This is what Marjorie would ask if we were really staying here for a vacation and not living here because of a house fire. If I were the version of myself who wore crewneck sweaters that cost seventy dollars and yoga pants that cost more than my clothes budget for entire years. If Beau was mine, the way

I'm beginning to think I belong to him. "Maybe—"

The scream from outside starts shrill, cuts off abruptly, and starts up again.

Paige.

I push my coffee onto the countertop so hard it tips over and run for the front door. She left it open. My heart beats high in my throat. My toe catches the doorjamb and I stumble out onto the porch, scanning for the woman in the nightgown, frantic that Paige is hurt. Footsteps behind me, heavy and uneven on the stairs. Beau's coming. "Jane—"

"Sweetheart."

Paige stands in the middle of the porch, her shoulders hunched forward. She clutches the clear bag the newspaper came in, a spray of plastic rising from two fists that haven't lost all their childhood chubbiness. Her chest heaves, and as I take the last step toward her, another scream tears out of her. "Jane," she screams. "Jane, Jane."

I turn her into my side and pull her with me. Across the porch.

Away from the thing that made her scream.

Beau barrels out the door as soon as we're out of the way and looks. "Christ." He picks his head up and scans around us. There's no one. There's no one in sight. His eyes land on the two of us. Paige, her face pressed into my belly, her whole body shaking.

"What was that?" Every word is interrupted with a sob. "What was it, Jane?"

She already saw it, so I won't lie. "It was a... an animal."

A dead rat. And not a rat that had crawled up from the ground and died of natural causes. Not a rat that had been brought to us as a gift from the kitten.

A murdered rat in its own pool of blood.

I meet Beau's eyes across the porch. There's fury in his expression. And fear. "Are you all right?" he asks, his voice rough. He sounds worried. More worried than I've ever heard him.

Because it wasn't just the rat. There was a note. It said *Jane*.

It was for me. It was meant for me to find and to see.

It was meant to make me afraid. And it's working.

I'm definitely not okay. I rub a hand down Paige's back, between her little shoulder blades. "We're going to be fine," I tell Beau in a level voice. "It was scary, but we're going to be fine."

The look on his face scares me more than the

rat. I can see him pulling away, building that wall between us. Here on the porch, with his body blocking the horrific sight from view. "It's time to go in." It sounds final, in that tone. As if we've finally come to the end of something. "We need to go inside. Right the fuck now."

CHAPTER TWENTY-ONE

Beau Rochester

J ANE TAKES PAIGE inside.

They take the first step through the front door and Paige starts to wail. It's worse than the screaming she did when we first arrived here. It's worse than the terrified screams that brought me running down the stairs. It reminds me of the way she cried after the wake, sobs consuming her whole body. Marjorie is there, her face white. The three of them go into the living room and Jane falls onto the couch, pulling Paige along with her.

What the fuck.

A dead rat. Out on the porch. For Jane.

Why?

The hair on the back of my neck pulls so tight it hurts. I can feel eyes on me from every angle but I can't see a damn person. Paige's howling slashes through the morning breeze again and again. It starts to taper off but the storm in my own head doesn't.

Joe Causey did this.

That's the logical conclusion. Causey did this. He put the rat there to terrify Jane into confessing something. He wants her to break down and admit she set the fire at the house. Or hell, he would probably be satisfied driving her away from me.

I can't even call the police. Causey *is* the police. Even if another officer takes the call, he'll be the one investigating his own damn crime.

Mateo meets me outside, quiet and calming in that way of his. "What can I do?" he asks.

"Bury it," I say, gritting my teeth against what I have to do. It will be a hell of a lot harder than digging a hole, but I can't put it off any longer.

"I checked the camera. Whoever it was concealed head to toe. They knew the doorbell was a camera, and they did it when it was dark out."

"Don't act as if it's a mystery," I say. "Joe Causey knows we have surveillance at the inn. He was pissed when he found out we recorded him."

A pause. "I'll handle this. What are you going to do about Jane?"

I haven't had any illusions about Jane. I'm dangerous to her. The boss who couldn't stay away from her. Even now, I don't want to stay away from her.

I want her in my house, in my bed.

"I'll do what I have to do," I say, though the words feel like shards of glass inside my throat. "Whatever it takes to keep her safe."

"You'll send her home." Mateo's staring at me, his jaw set.

"No, I won't." My leg feels like it's crumbling from being out here. My thigh bone could snap in half. I ignore it. "How the hell would that help anything? I can't protect her in Houston."

Mateo's eyes widen. "You're shitting me. You *have* to send her home."

"She's not safe on her own."

"She's not safe with *you*," he bursts out, barely managing to keep his voice low. "You're playing games with her. She's already your employee. And a decade younger than you. Now things are getting dangerous, and you're going keep her around so you can fuck her?"

The words land like a goddamn arrow. Right in the center. Bullseye. No, she's not safe with me. It doesn't mean I can let her go. "I can't do a damn thing for her if I send her out of here."

"That's all you can do for her. Damn it, Beau. That's all you can do. Give Jane her life back.

Stop stealing it from her. Don't be a selfish asshole about this."

I square off with him. "Don't tell me what's good for her."

"How dare you risk her?" He looks pained to say it. "How dare you drag her into your shit? I always knew you had baggage, and I accepted it. I also accepted that Emily knew what she was doing with you, but this is different. Jane is innocent. She's young."

"She's—"

"She's too goddamn young to be embroiled in this." Mateo's voice softens. "I know it blows. But you have to send her back home. Anything else happens to her, and you'll be on the hook for it. Maybe not legally, but morally. You won't be able to live with yourself."

"I—" He's right. That's what hurts more than everything else. That's what's stopping my goddamn heart. "I know. Yes. You're right."

Mateo nods. "I'll take her to the airport. You have to go tell her."

I go back through the door and into the living room.

Paige is quiet now, but it's only because she's cried herself to sleep in Jane's lap. Her arms cradle the morning paper in its plastic bag. Jane leans against the back of the couch and runs her fingers through Paige's hair. She swallows hard. "Do you think we should call—"

"We're not calling anyone." We can't. Joe Causey did this, and Joe Causey will know if we call the police. What good would it do? I have to resolve this on my own. "Jane."

"Yeah?" She glances down at Paige in her lap. A dead rat left for her, and she's more worried for Paige than herself. God, what have I been thinking, letting her stay here? I should have known better than that. I should have known from the first night she walked into my house that it wouldn't be simple. *My love is dangerous.* That's been proven today.

"It's time to go."

Her brow furrows, but she doesn't stop stroking Paige's hair. "What do you mean?"

"You need to leave."

Causey wouldn't come after a child. He wouldn't come after his own niece. He doesn't realize that he's hurting Paige anyway. He has no idea the pain this will cause. He's blinded by spite, and something has pushed him over the edge. I don't care to analyze it now. All I know is that I have to get her away from this place. When Jane's somewhere safe, I can make Joe believe I don't care about her. I'll make sure the investigation finds the real arsonist here in Maine.

Jane shakes her head. She doesn't understand. "Go upstairs? Is someone coming to take care of the rat?"

"No. You're going home. Back to Houston. You need to pack your things and get ready to go. Mateo will take you to the airport."

"Beau." A shocked whisper. "What are you saying? I'm not leaving."

It's a struggle to keep my voice in check. I don't want to startle Paige out of her sleep. Enough has happened to that girl to last several lifetimes. I'm about to make it worse. Paige might never forgive me for sending Jane away. *I had no other choice* won't be a good enough explanation. It hardly sounds like one in my own head.

But it's the only way I can keep her safe.

"You're going on the first flight out."

A tear slips down Jane's cheek, but she doesn't sob. She barely moves. "You wouldn't do this. I know you care about me. I know you love me."

"I do love you." It's a knife to the throat to say the words to her like this. Damn you, Rochester. Damn you for letting it get so out of control. "That doesn't change anything."

Jane's mouth drops open. "It's everything."

"It doesn't." I'm an asshole, standing over her to say this. I should get down on my knees and hold her hand. I should beg. But if Jane sees that kind of softness from me, she won't leave. And she has to leave. She has to leave today. Before this goes any further. I take out my phone. "People who love each other don't always end up together."

Jane blinks and another tear falls down her cheek. She shakes her head. Christ, I can see it in her eyes. What she's thinking. She's thinking this is about Emily, and the fact that I didn't get what I wanted from that relationship.

She's wrong. This isn't about Emily, and can't be about Emily. I was never going to get what I wanted from any relationship with Emily because what I want is Jane. I just didn't know it yet. She hadn't walked into my life yet. I couldn't have known.

"What are you doing?"

"I'm booking you a flight."

Jane allows herself one single, stifled sob, but then she swallows hard and makes the rest of them disappear. "I'm not leaving you," she says, her eyes on the ceiling. But then she brings them back to me. "I'm not leaving Paige."

"You are." My only consideration for the

flight is how quickly it can get her back to Houston. "Because you don't work for me anymore."

Her eyes go wide. The very first day I met Jane Mendoza, I was casual about my power over her. You're locked in for a year. I'm not. I can fire you anytime I want. She must be remembering it now. It's still true. According to the terms of our contract, Jane is an at-will employee. The agency contract is designed in everyone's favor but hers. I only have to gesture at dissatisfaction to fire her. They don't even require a written explanation.

All it takes is one email. I tap it out and hit send.

"Your flight is booked. I've notified the agency that your employment has been terminated effective immediately. I'm wiring the full payment now."

Jane lifts one hand from Paige's small back and brushes away the tears from her cheeks. "Maybe this is your chance."

"For what?" This isn't my chance to do anything except keep drawing in breath after painful breath. This is the last thing I ever wanted to say to her. The last goddamn thing.

"At Emily," she says, shrugging one shoulder in a way that's so nonchalant it crushes the air out of my lungs. "If she's still alive, you could be with the woman you wanted all along."

"Jane."

She ignores me. Jane eases herself out from under Paige, who turns to face the back of the couch and keeps sleeping. She'll be awake soon, and I'll have to explain why Jane's leaving. Jane runs a hand along her shoulder, then straightens up and faces me. "I don't have anything to take with me. Everything burned in the fire."

Christ. "Take your clothes. And your phone. I'm not sending you away empty-handed."

Jane looks down at herself like she's seeing the clothes for the first time. She lets out a laugh that sounds almost bitter. My chest squeezes. That bitterness is a painfully unfamiliar sound. "I'm sure I'll fit right in at home."

CHAPTER TWENTY-TWO

Jane Mendoza

THE HOUSTON AIRPORT teems with kids on spring break. Some of them, older groups, heading to beaches. Others with small children, already decked out in Disney gear.

A small girl races into her mother's arms, and my chest pangs. I miss Paige. It's only been hours since I gave her a hug goodbye, but it hurts. She refused to move. Or speak. Or acknowledge what I was telling her. It feels awful having surprised her with the news.

I'll never see her again.

Kitten wriggled away from my hug, not understanding why I was holding her so tight or why my eyes were leaking. I'll never see her again either.

Sunglasses disguise my puffy, red eyes. No one questions why I'm wearing them indoors. I head away from the gate with my luggage trailing behind me. Outside there are people hugging and exclaiming as they meet their loved ones. I'm looking for a red Nissan Versa according to the app, but the map says it's still fifteen minutes away.

"Jane."

I glance up to see Noah walking toward me. "What are you doing here?"

"You sent me your flight number. I couldn't wait to see you."

He wraps me in a warm, familiar embrace, and I shudder out a breath. I'm not sure if I'll be able to talk about it without breaking down in tears. Public scenes are not exactly my thing. I don't want to cry in front of all these strangers. I don't even want to cry in front of Noah.

"You want to talk about it?" he asks, his words soft.

We've been through a lot together, but I don't even know where to begin with this. I want to rail and scream and sob—but most of all, I don't want to hurt him. Noah. The one guy who has been with me for all this time. He doesn't need to know that I slept with Beau. "I got fired."

"Good," he says. "It wasn't safe there for you."

Beau's words ring in my head. *My love is dan-*

gerous. I didn't believe him at first, but by the end I did. Maine isn't safe for me. Is it safe for him? For Paige? I'm not there to protect them anymore. It hits me like a knife in the chest. "Right."

He taps the side of my sunglasses. "These hiding something?"

I glance over his shoulder to where his ancient truck waits against the curb. "I still don't understand how you're here. Don't you have to work right now?"

"I traded shifts, and no, you're not going to change the subject."

A shaky exhale. "They still don't know who set the fire, but it doesn't matter. I'm not there anymore. And I really, really—" My voice breaks. "Really care about that little girl. I screwed up. I got too close. You told me not to, but I did it anyway."

"He touched you."

So much for keeping secrets. Apparently even wearing dark sunglasses and wrapped in a large sweater, I'm an open book. "I'm sorry, Noah."

"Don't be fucking sorry. He took advantage of his position."

"I can't listen to another rant about rich people right now. It's not... me. It's not my life. I got confused there for a minute, I got caught up in something, but it's over now. I'm back where I belong."

He studies me. "You never did fit in with us, Jane."

"Don't." I never fit in anywhere. I never had a family, and probably never will.

"I thought you were gone for good."

"Bad luck for you."

He slings his arm around my head, pulling me in for a kiss on the cheek. "No, babe. It's good luck for me, shit luck for you, but the world has never played fair, has it?"

There's shouting around us as people argue about where they can stop their car. There's a jam of vehicles, a mixture of people picking up their loved ones and Uber drivers. A couple of traffic cops wearing bright orange vests wave people angrily to move on.

There are "no stopping" signs posted everywhere, though how people will pick up passengers without stopping, I don't know.

It's a broken system.

I remember Noah saying something to me once. If the only punishment is a fine, then the rule only exists for poor people. I shrugged at the time, but now I understand better, now that I've lived under Beau Rochester's roof for six months.

He would have ignored the signs about stopping. They probably wouldn't ticket a Porsche SUV, but if they did, losing a few hundred dollars means nothing to him.

They would, however, fine a scratched-up old truck.

I could pay the fine with the money Basset Agency deposited into my bank account this morning. I stared at it for a solid five minutes before I could move. I've never seen that many commas in my balance. He paid the full amount even though I didn't work the entire year under the terms of the contract. It doesn't make me feel any better. If anything, I feel worse.

The money feels dirty now.

"Let's go," I say, linking my arm in Noah's.

We need to move along. I need to move along, too. Get over Beau Rochester. Forget about Paige. I won't ever see Kitten again, either.

Tears roll down my cheeks.

The smell of exhaust floods my mouth. I'm not sure it's possible for me to move on. We climb in and slam the doors shut, but the shouting continues. Someone in a BMW is arguing with someone in a Ford. They are both waving their hands wildly.

Noah turns the key. The truck rumbles to life.

We drive past them and ease into the flow of traffic, entering the heart of Houston, but my soul is still in Maine.

CHAPTER TWENTY-THREE

Beau Rochester

THE MINUTE JANE'S car pulls away, Paige goes silent.

Her face turns red. She stands at the sidewalk, watching the taillights until it turns out of sight. Her shoulders sag. Her teeth click together, but her chin doesn't wobble. All the color drains from her face except two red splotches high on her cheeks.

She stands there, staring at the empty turn of the road.

"Paige, it's time to go inside."

She ignores me.

I ask her. I coax her. I command her. None of it works.

She stands there like an angry, grieving statue. At first I attempt to talk her down. When that doesn't work I sit on the steps of the front porch.

If she needs time, I'll give her time.

Fifteen minutes turns into thirty.

Thirty minutes turns into forty five.

At an hour I consider picking her up bodily and putting her inside the house. I've never put my hands on her in anger, and I don't feel angry now, only a deep concern for her well being. I know what's happening isn't good. It isn't right, but I also don't know the best way to handle it. What if she needs this time to process?

Technically she isn't harming herself.

It's a beautiful windy day. Seagulls call from the ocean. There's a shout of someone on the beach. The faint rumble of the ocean underlies all of it.

An hour and twenty minutes. That's how long it takes Paige to break.

She does get her stubbornness from the Rochester side of the family, after all.

She whirls to face me, her hands balled into fists at her side. "She said she wasn't leaving. She promised, she promised, she promised."

She levels the accusation at me, and she's right to do it. I'm the one who made this happen. I'm the one who made Jane leave. "Sometimes plans have to change, sweetheart."

Her blue eyes stay on mine as she processes

what I've said.

My head pounds. I'm not sure what started the headache in the first place. Paige's screaming this morning? Or did it begin yesterday, when we were waiting for Joe Causey to show up to the inn? Or did it start well before that, when I was pinned under a collapsed beam in my own house, looking into Jane's eyes and pleading with her to live?

I have no goddamn idea. I've lost track.

"She said she wasn't leaving?" Now it's more of a question.

I didn't think my heart could be reduced to more ash. I was wrong. And now I'm wishing Jane was here. She'd know what to say to Paige, whose distress comes off her in waves.

The sight of her brokenhearted and wailing is bad enough.

This stoic silence is worse.

"I know." What the hell kinds of things did Jane say to soothe her? I can't retreat to the old habits I had before. Not now that I have better methods. But I don't have time to study now. The test is here already. "You wanted her to stay, but she had to go. It's the only way she could be safe, and we want her to be safe, don't we?"

Paige narrows her eyes. To my endless shame,

I wasn't always like this with her. The two of us were caught in the same storm on different boats. If she called me out on it now, I'd deserve it. "Why couldn't we keep her safe here?"

It's too much to explain. Too much to explain the dark, terrible history that makes her mere presence in Maine a risk. How can I tell her that her uncle Joe wants to lock Jane up? "It's a grown-up problem, Paige. I know it's hard to accept, but I need you to trust me."

Her chin quivers, but Paige keeps her teeth clenched tight together. I would feel better if she punched and screamed and cried. If she raged against me.

Light flashes off a car's side mirror at the corner, and both of us turn toward it.

If it's Mateo bringing Jane back, then I'll accept it. I'm not sure I'd have the strength to send her away again. I would have to keep my body between her and whatever threat comes to us. I'll stand in front of Paige and Jane for the rest of my goddamn life if that's what it takes.

The car comes fully into view.

It's not Mateo's. Disappointment beats in my chest, even as I know it's for the best.

It's a black detective's car with Joe Causey in the driver's seat.

I'm going to kill him. Maim him at the very least.

The front door of the inn opens. Marjorie must have seen the car. She looks worried. "Paige? Would you like something to drink? Some cookies, maybe?"

She looks vaguely interested at the mention of cookies, but her frown doesn't budge. I think it'll be there for a long time. At least as long as Jane lived with us. Maybe longer.

The car pulls into the inn's drive. Of course it does. After the way Jane's interview went, he won't be coming here unless it's to bother me. Well, he can't touch her anymore.

"Go in and have some cookies," I tell Paige. "I'll be right there. Okay?"

She takes a deep, shaky breath. "Do you promise?"

Jane made similar promises to her, and I forced her not to keep them. If I were a better man, I'd be honest with Paige. No one can guarantee they'll stay in your life. No one can really promise you forever. "I promise."

Paige runs past me into the house.

The only relief I feel is at the sound of the door closing behind me. Joe pulls his car onto the inn's driveway. He climbs out of the car and heads straight for me.

"You've done enough, don't you think?" The acid tone probably isn't right for a cop, but I don't care. Jane's absence is like an open wound. My fucked-up leg throbs. My head aches. "You want another interview, then I need advance warning."

"I don't need to talk to Paige or Jane. I need to talk to you."

"I've answered your questions."

He comes to a stop in front of me on the sidewalk, and I get my first good look at him. Pale and sweaty. Not the cocky bastard who came to sit across the table during the interviews. He rubs at the back of his neck, looking uncertain, shell shocked.

What the hell is happening right now? Is this some kind of trick?

"Tell me why you're here before I help you get the hell out of my sight." I need to go somewhere alone, if only for a few minutes. I feel like I'm having a goddamn heart attack.

"I've got proof," Joe says, almost to himself.

"Of what?" I spit back at him. "Proof about Jane? Too late. I sent her away. You don't get to harass her anymore. No more messages on the front porch. Leave us the fuck alone."

He blinks at me. "What are you talking about?"

Something's wrong. He's not just pale with a sheen of sweat on his forehead. His pale blue eyes have taken on a gray cast in the daylight, like a ghost walked through them and stole the color. He looks haunted. "I'm talking about Jane. I'm talking about everything you've done to scare her. To intimidate her. An innocent goddamn woman."

Joe shakes his head. It's like he hasn't heard a word I've said. "No. Not about Jane. I'm talking about Emily. She's alive, damn it."

My stomach drops. "Don't play this fucking game with me."

"I can show you."

I'm already shaking my head. "Have you gone insane? I don't even know whether you believe what you're saying. I know you loved your sister, but you've got to let her go."

"Here." Joe looks me in the eye. Cold fear drops over me like a sheet of frigid ocean water. He could arrest me on suspicion of murder if they found a body. He's suspicious enough to do it right here on the sidewalk. What that would do to Paige—"They found her here, Beau. Alive."

He seems serious. Either that or he's batshit

crazy.

Or he's telling the truth.

All this time there was this uneasy possibility of a ghost. As if she's returned from the dead to haunt us. Impossible, of course. I don't believe in ghosts. "Where?" I find myself asking.

"Here in Eben Cape. Downtown." A hollow laugh. "She's been right under my nose the entire time. I'm not sure I'd have believed it if I hadn't seen the video myself."

A part of me thought it would be easier if they'd found a body. We would have more closure. Paige would have more closure, even if the answer hurt like a motherfucker. It's going to hurt anyway. Because someday I'm going to have to tell Paige what happened to her mother. That she faked her own death, apparently. It still seems impossible.

"How did they find her?" I blink my way back to looking him in the eye. The sun feels too hot on my skin now. Burning, like a house fire. "And what do you mean, proof?"

Joe takes his phone out of his pocket, swipes across the screen a few times, and hands it to me. "This footage was taken by a security camera in one of the shops early this morning. The owner followed the case when we were actively searching for her. He called the tip line because he remembered our original request for sightings of women matching Emily's description."

At first there's no one on the screen. Just a wide-angle view of the front window of the bakery downtown. The footage is from early in the morning, according to the time stamp. About ten seconds in, the front door opens and the baker comes through. He walks past the counter and disappears from view.

And then a lady strolls in front of the window from the left side of the screen.

It's her.

I know it instantly from her profile and the way she walks. Emily wears a long white dress with small straps. She walks in front of the bakery's second window and pauses.

My vision blanks out. All this time, I've been wondering. Entertaining the possibilities. Trying to decide which one would be less earth-shattering to discover. This one's it.

My lips have gone numb. She didn't die in the boating accident.

If Joe has proof she's alive, she's been alive all this time.

Why hasn't she come for her already? If Emily is alive, why hasn't she come for Paige?

Emily could never resist a bakery. She loved cinnamon rolls and doughnuts and these little pastries with custard inside. The Emily in the security film leans into the window and cups her hands around her eyes to see through. It gives the camera a perfect shot of her face.

It's her. It's her. It's her.

I shove the phone back into Joe's hand. "Where has she been all this time?"

"I don't know." I never thought I'd see Joe like this again after the funeral. He looks lost. Bereft. "We have an APB out for her, but this all happened so fast."

"Goddamn it, she's not a ghost. If this video is real, she's a real woman walking around Eben Cape. Find her." It's not fair to snarl at Joe for this, but for all the other things he's done—he deserves it. But it doesn't register with him. He doesn't bristle or tell me to shut the hell up or threaten me with jail time. He just stares off through the side lawn and out over the ocean.

He thought his sister died out on the water. He blamed me for her death, when she wasn't really dead at all. "That's the thing," he says finally. "She doesn't want to be found."

If Emily's alive, my custody of Paige is in jeopardy.

A fierce protectiveness comes up like a shield over my heart. What the hell am I supposed to do if Emily emerges now? Hand Paige over? She's become mine. My niece.

Maybe even my daughter.

CHAPTER TWENTY-FOUR

Jane Mendoza

NOAH PULLS UP in front of my old apartment. The building sags where the foundation has dropped. There's a hard line of broken bricks down the center. You can feel the shift in the concrete from the inside. Sometimes water pools up from the bottom, spilling into the brown carpet. Our stairs are right in front of the dumpsters, which is great for taking out the trash. Not so great for the smell. It's not a pretty place, but it's home.

He's dropped me off here hundreds of times before. It should be the most natural thing in the world. Instead it feels foreign, like a place I no longer belong.

"It's a good thing they didn't sublet your spot," he says. "It would have been a pain in the ass to find a new place. Especially on such short notice."

Probably about as painful as having to call my roommate and explain that I'm back in town months early. My old room is still available, with its top-bunk twin bed. I won't need a full half of the rickety dresser. I didn't bring all the clothes Mateo bought for me. Only what would fit in the small rolling suitcase. It's a Louis Vuitton suitcase that a guest once left in the Lighthouse Inn. Marjorie found it in storage. Imagine being rich enough that you can forget a four thousand dollar suitcase and not bother to send for it. Between the luggage, the clothes inside, and my phone, I'm like a completely different person than the woman who left Houston.

"Yeah. It's better this way." A lie I'll keep repeating until it becomes the truth. If it ever does.

It's better this way, a million miles away from Beau Rochester. Never seeing Paige grow up. Not having the family that had seemed for one shining second like I belonged.

I open the door to his car and get out before I can beg him to drive me back to the airport. It hurts so bad to be here, alone and adrift. My chest aches from it. And everything is wrong. My clothes are too hot for Houston. Ironically the clothes are more expensive than anything I could have purchased here, but the fabric is too thick. They're not made for heat like this. The yoga pants that felt so good in Maine make my legs feel constricted now.

Noah gets out with me and comes around to hand me my bag. "You sure you don't want me to come in? I could stay with you for a while. Get you settled in."

We used to hang out for hours at a time without any particular plan. We'd binge-watch something on the Netflix we shared with the rest of my roommates. Or we'd lie in bed watching TikTok, showing each other the funniest ones. I can't imagine doing those things now. It feels like a different woman did those. I don't know who I am now, but I know that I've changed. "I'm sure," I say, giving him a smile to soften the rejection. "I'll text you later."

He puts his arms around me for a quick squeeze and kisses the top of my head. His arms around me feel wrong. Not because he's too rough or anything. He's just not Beau Rochester. "People like you and me, we don't stay in one place for long."

If you leave early enough, you won't miss them when you're gone.

But I already know it didn't work. I'll miss them forever. "I know."

He waits in his car while I walk up to the door. This is an old habit, too. Noah and I have never lived in the safest neighborhoods. We don't just drive off before the other person is safely inside.

The key sticks in the door, and it takes several turns before I can get the lock to pop open. Once it does, I turn around and wave to Noah. He waves back. It's a minute more before he actually drives away. I step inside the familiar crowded vestibule with the peeling laminate floor and the coat tree that's packed with hoodies, umbrellas, and backpacks.

I've walked through here a thousand times, but it feels smaller now. I've gotten used to the Coach House. I've gotten used to the inn. Which is unfortunate, because I live here now. This is my life. I'll use the money from Beau to go to college, but I'm not going to live a life of luxury.

The heat from outside has crept in with me.

It feels suffocating.

No. I can still breathe. In and out. I force my breathing to even. It's hard because my chest hurts so much. I would love a few minutes to cry in peace. I didn't want to cry in front of Noah in the airport, and I don't want to cry in front of any of my roommates now. Though it sounds quiet enough in the apartment that everyone may be at work. It is the middle of the day, after all. Some of them are in college, some are working. We're all busy, only catching each other at night, usually. I'm sure they'll want me to share everything tonight, but I can't imagine opening up about Beau and Paige. It would be like opening a wound.

Nobody's on the couch, or in the lumpy arm-chair in the corner, and I let out a big breath.

I might not have to cry in front of anyone after all.

The pitted paint on the walls is the same. The ratty carpet is the same. The tiny kitchen table with its four chairs—not big enough for all of us at the same time—the same. It's like the stories in the library books I'd escape into. I'm the one who's different now. I just didn't expect to be this different. It's like trying to squeeze into clothes two sizes too small.

I roll my bag over the threadbare carpet to the second door on the left. It's an old, old habit to stop outside the door and listen. Best not to walk inside if two of my roommates are having an argument. Or having makeup sex. If that's happening now, I'll find another time to go in.

No voices filter out into the hall. No creaking floors underneath someone's chair. No footsteps coming across the living room. Nothing.

My second key fits in the lock. Each of the bedrooms has its own lock separate from the deadbolt. When you share an apartment with six other people, things are bound to go missing. The keys are a way to minimize that.

I shoulder the door open and roll my bag inside. The hallway here is so narrow it feels like the walls are pressing into my shoulders from both sides, but they're not.

I close the door behind me.

And freeze.

There's something expectant about the air.

Like someone's just stepped out. Or just stepped in?

I know better than to let myself dwell in regret about Maine. The past is the past. When it's time to go, you pack up your clothes and go to the next place. But it's not regret, exactly, that makes my heart feel bruised. It's how different this place is from when I left.

Or maybe it's how different I am here from the woman I was there.

I've survived places that didn't fit before.

I'll survive again.

A few minutes alone. That's all I need. After that, I'll be okay.

There's a woman sitting at my small desk chair, the one with the broken arm. It always slides down when I'm in the middle of concentrating.

Of course, this woman isn't studying.

She's not a roommate.

No. She doesn't even belong in Houston.

She turns her head and smiles at me.

Emily Rochester smiles at me.

My heart slams into my throat, cold adrenaline raking down my spine. I recognize her from a photo I found in a diary. I know her face. I left Maine because we thought Detective Joe Causey was after me. Does he know his sister is alive?

She's beautiful, and very much not a ghost.

Her smile is perfectly pleasant. Perfectly poised. "Hello, Jane."

THE END

Thank you so much for reading!

The final book in the Rochester trilogy comes out next. BEST KEPT SECRET is the breathtaking conclusion to Beau and Jane's explosive love story...

The secrets haunting Beau Rochester come alive.

He doesn't deserve happiness, but he holds it in his hands. A woman he loves. A child. The past threatens to rip them away. He risks losing them forever.

Jane Mendoza is determined to protect the people she loves from every threat—the mysterious arsonist, the corrupt police force. The darkest danger comes from a place she never expects.

She risks more than her newfound family. She risks her life.

And I'm thrilled to offer a sneak peek of THE
PAWN, the USA Today bestselling full-length
dark contemporary novel about revenge and
seduction in the game of love…

"Wickedly brilliant, dark and addictive!"

– Jodi Ellen Malpas, #1 New York Times
bestselling author

✧   ✧   ✧

WIND WHIPS AROUND my ankles, flapping the
bottom of my black trench coat. Beads of
moisture form on my eyelashes. In the short walk
from the cab to the stoop, my skin has slicked
with humidity left by the rain.

Carved vines and ivy leaves decorate the ornate wooden door.

I have some knowledge of antique pieces, but
I can't imagine the price tag on this one—
especially exposed to the elements and the whims
of vandals. I suppose even criminals know enough
to leave the Den alone.

Officially the Den is a gentlemen's club, the
old-world kind with cigars and private invitations.

Unofficially it's a collection of the most powerful men in Tanglewood. Dangerous men. Criminals, even if they wear a suit while breaking the law.

A heavy brass knocker in the shape of a fierce lion warns away any visitors. I'm desperate enough to ignore that warning. My heart thuds in my chest and expands out, pulsing in my fingers, my toes. Blood rushes through my ears, drowning out the whoosh of traffic behind me.

I grasp the thick ring and knock—once, twice.

Part of me fears what will happen to me behind that door. A bigger part of me is afraid the door won't open at all. I can't see any cameras set into the concrete enclave, but they have to be watching. Will they recognize me? I'm not sure it would help if they did. Probably best that they see only a desperate girl, because that's all I am now.

The softest scrape comes from the door. Then it opens.

I'm struck by his eyes, a deep amber color— like expensive brandy and almost translucent. My breath catches in my throat, lips frozen against words like *please* and *help*. Instinctively I know they won't work; this isn't a man given to mercy. The tailored cut of his shirt, its sleeves carelessly rolled up, tells me he'll extract a price. One I can't afford to pay.

There should have been a servant, I thought. A butler. Isn't that what fancy gentlemen's clubs have? Or maybe some kind of a security guard. Even our house had a housekeeper answer the door—at least, before. Before we fell from grace.

Before my world fell apart.

The man makes no move to speak, to invite me in or turn me away. Instead he stares at me with vague curiosity, with a trace of pity, the way one might watch an animal in the zoo. That might be how the whole world looks to these men, who have more money than God, more power than the president.

That might be how I looked at the world, before.

My throat feels tight, as if my body fights this move, even while my mind knows it's the only option. "I need to speak with Damon Scott."

Scott is the most notorious loan shark in the city. He deals with large sums of money, and nothing less will get me through this. We have been introduced, and he left polite society by the time I was old enough to attend events regularly. There were whispers, even then, about the young man with ambition. Back then he had ties to the underworld—and now he's its king.

One thick eyebrow rises. "What do you want

with him?"

A sense of familiarity fills the space between us even though I know we haven't met. This man is a stranger, but he looks at me as if he wants to know me. He looks at me as if he already does. There's an intensity to his eyes when they sweep over my face, as firm and as telling as a touch.

"I need…" My heart thuds as I think about all the things I need—a rewind button. One person in the city who doesn't hate me by name alone. "I need a loan."

He gives me a slow perusal, from the nervous slide of my tongue along my lips to the high neckline of my clothes. I tried to dress professionally—a black cowl-necked sweater and pencil skirt. His strange amber gaze unbuttons my coat, pulls away the expensive cotton, tears off the fabric of my bra and panties. He sees right through me, and I shiver as a ripple of awareness runs over my skin.

I've met a million men in my life. Shaken hands. Smiled. I've never felt as seen through as I do right now. Never felt like someone has turned me inside out, every dark secret exposed to the harsh light. He sees my weaknesses, and from the cruel set of his mouth, he likes them.

His lids lower. "And what do you have for

collateral?"

Nothing except my word. That wouldn't be worth anything if he knew my name. I swallow past the lump in my throat. "I don't know."

Nothing.

He takes a step forward, and suddenly I'm crowded against the brick wall beside the door, his large body blocking out the warm light from inside. He feels like a furnace in front of me, the heat of him in sharp contrast to the cold brick at my back. "What's your name, girl?"

The word *girl* is a slap in the face. I force myself not to flinch, but it's hard. Everything about him overwhelms me—his size, his low voice. "I'll tell Mr. Scott my name."

In the shadowed space between us, his smile spreads, white and taunting. The pleasure that lights his strange yellow eyes is almost sensual, as if I caressed him. "You'll have to get past me."

My heart thuds. He likes that I'm challenging him, and God, that's even worse. What if I've already failed? I'm free-falling, tumbling, turning over without a single hope to anchor me. Where will I go if he turns me away? What will happen to my father?

"Let me go," I whisper, but my hope fades fast.

His eyes flash with warning. "Little Avery James, all grown up."

A small gasp resounds in the space between us. He already knows my name. That means he knows who my father is. He knows what he's done. Denials rush to my throat, pleas for understanding. The hard set of his eyes, the broad strength of his shoulders tells me I won't find any mercy here.

I square my shoulders. I'm desperate but not broken. "If you know my name, you know I have friends in high places. Connections. A history in this city. That has to be worth something. That's my collateral."

Those connections might not even take my call, but I have to try something. I don't know if it will be enough for a loan or even to get me through the door. Even so, a faint feeling of family pride rushes over my skin. Even if he turns me away, I'll hold my head high.

Golden eyes study me. Something about the way he said *little Avery James* felt familiar, but I've never seen this man. At least I don't think we've met. Something about the otherworldly glow of those eyes whispers to me, like a melody I've heard before.

On his driver's license it probably says something mundane, like brown. But that word can never encompass the way his eyes seem almost luminous, orbs of amber that hold the secrets of the universe. *Brown* can never describe the deep golden hue of them, the indelible opulence in his fierce gaze.

"Follow me," he says.

Relief courses through me, flooding numb limbs, waking me up enough that I wonder what I'm doing here. These aren't men, they're animals. They're predators, and I'm prey. Why would I willingly walk inside?

What other choice do I have?

I step over the veined marble threshold.

The man closes the door behind me, shutting out the rain and the traffic, the entire city disappeared in one soft turn of the lock. Without another word he walks down the hall, deeper into the shadows. I hurry to follow him, my chin held high, shoulders back, for all the world as if I were an invited guest. Is this how the gazelle feels when she runs over the plains, a study in grace, poised for her slaughter?

The entire world goes black behind the staircase, only breath, only bodies in the dark. Then he opens another thick wooden door, revealing a dimly lit room of cherrywood and cut crystal, of leather and smoke. Barely I see dark eyes, dark suits. Dark men.

I have the sudden urge to hide behind the man with the golden eyes. He's wide and tall, with hands that could wrap around my waist. He's a giant of a man, rough-hewn and hard as stone.

Except he's not here to protect me.

He could be the most dangerous of all.

Want to read more? Order The Pawn from Amazon, Barnes & Noble, Apple Books, or Kobo.

Books by Skye Warren

Endgame Trilogy & more books in Tanglewood

The Pawn

The Knight

The Castle

The King

The Queen

Escort

Survival of the Richest

The Evolution of Man

Mating Theory

The Bishop

North Security Trilogy & more North brothers

Overture

Concerto

Sonata

Audition

Diamond in the Rough

Silver Lining

Gold Mine

Finale

Chicago Underground series

Rough

Hard

Fierce

Wild

Dirty

Secret

Sweet

Deep

Stripped series

Tough Love

Love the Way You Lie

Better When It Hurts

Even Better

Pretty When You Cry

Caught for Christmas

Hold You Against Me

To the Ends of the Earth

**For a complete listing of Skye Warren books,
visit
www.skyewarren.com/books**

About the Author

Skye Warren is the New York Times bestselling author of dangerous romance. Her books have sold over one million copies. She makes her home in Texas with her loving family, sweet dogs, and evil cat.

Sign up for Skye's newsletter:
www.skyewarren.com/newsletter

Like Skye Warren on Facebook:
facebook.com/skyewarren

Join Skye Warren's Dark Room reader group:
skyewarren.com/darkroom

Follow Skye Warren on Instagram:
instagram.com/skyewarrenbooks

Visit Skye's website for her current booklist:
www.skyewarren.com

Copyright

This is a work of fiction. Any resemblance to actual persons, living or dead, business establishments, events or locales is entirely coincidental. All rights reserved. Except for use in a review, the reproduction or use of this work in any part is forbidden without the express written permission of the author.